MOGZILLA

Threadneedle

First published by Mogzilla in 2017.

Paperback edition:

ISBN: 9781906132057

Printed in the UK

www.londondeep.co.uk

www.paulmcgrory.co.uk

http://club.creativewritingclub.co.uk

Recap

The *London Deep* series is set in the near future in a flooded London where rival police forces for kids and grown ups compete to keep the peace. Jemima Mallard's father is a Chief Inspector in the APD (Adult Police Department).

In the book 1, *London Deep*, Jem broke so many laws that her father couldn't help her. Arrested by a YPD (Youth Police Defender) officer called Nick, she made a bargain. In exchange for a pardon, she helped the YPD to track down a criminal organisation called *Father Thames,* only to discover that her own mother was one of its leaders!

In book 2, *Father Thames,* Londoners were amazed when armed invaders appeared in warships. The strangers demanded that London send them workers for their 'Stormfather'. But the Stormfather turned out to be an ancient wind turbine. With the help of an islander called Harfleur, Jem and her father managed to get the wind farm generating priceless electricity again.

Threadneedle

THE YPD's SUPREME MANDER ADDRESSED THE MEETING.

Chapter 1: Charger

THREE WEEKS EARLIER..

"For Lud's sake!" muttered Jem as she peered through the crowd. "What's keeping my father?" Grizzled fishermen smoked and joked whilst merchants weighed their catches. Workers waited in gangs, ready to shift crates for the right price. Busy hands shifted cargo from containers. In the last two months, the port of Charger had tripled in size. The place was buzzing, but not from all of this human activity. The hum came from the power lines that stretched above Jem's head. The electricity grumbled as it creaked through the thick copper cables. Jemima felt the deep thrum. It had overtones at 1.17 Hz, roughly the same frequency as her heartbeat.

Jem pointed towards the row of charging shacks. In the six months since she'd first come to the island, a complex economy had bloomed. New charging shops were opening up every day. Only the bite of the wind remained constant. Rival outlets like Hali's Zap and Motherload competed to offer the cheapest electricity. The stranger trudged off, striking the dead tazor battery with the bottom of his fist.

If people had default personality settings, Jemima Mallard's would be stuck somewhere between offended and irritated. Her father was late, again. Jem sighed, her dad was about as much use as a flat tazor.

"Sorry I'm late luv," called a familiar voice.

Jemima's father had an apologetic look, even when he wasn't sorry about anything. He rolled his eyes and shivered.

"It's this blooming gale, nearly blew me back to London!"

Father and daughter were joined by a tall girl who held a harpoon in her tattooed hand. Jem noticed that the 'poon had a battery in the hilt. Everything was wired these days.

A 'permafrown' had been lingering on Jem's face for weeks. She'd planned frantically to avoid this meeting. The thought of standing here, next to THEM made her want to jump off the pier and sink. If her idiot father had got out of his bunk earlier this morning, they'd already be sailing back to London by now.

"Morning," said Nick enthusiastically.

Jem didn't answer. Harfleur filled the silence in a confident way.

"We missed you two at the meeting last night," she observed.

"Sorry luv but meetings aren't really my thing," said Mallard.

Really? You've been sailing a desk for years, thought Jem.

"More mercs turned up," explained Nick.

He wasn't sure whether 'merc' stood for merchant or 'mercenary'. Either way, they were as popular as a land mine at a beach party.

"What happened?" asked Mallard.

"We could have used your support," said Harfleur.

Nick sighed as he explained what had happened last night.

"There were three of them...." he began...

Nick eyed the mercs with the confidence of a man with a fully charged tazor hidden under his coat. These meetings were getting more and more unruly. At first many of the islanders had been too shy to attend but they'd taken to democracy like sharks to bloody water. You couldn't blame them for wanting to protect their island, Nick thought. Six months ago, when he had arrived, it was just a rock sticking up from an obscure patch of ocean. Since they'd got their wind farm turning again and the first lights had gone on, every islander had become rich beyond the dreams of Londoners. The islanders didn't know it yet, but news of their discovery was leaking like gas from a holed fuel tank.

"We've come to make our case," announced the tallest Merc.

"Sharks!" cried a voice from the middle of the hall. "We all know what you want. And the answer is still no!"

"No sale!" screamed a furious lady, waving her charge key.

"It looks like no one wants to sell their electricity shares. You'll have to offer your services elsewhere."

Cheers of approval rang around the hall.

The big merc stared at Nick through eyes that looked too small for his face. Nick saw the muscles under the merc's long coat and wished he could move his tazor setting up a few clicks. This guy was built like an oil tanker.

"Is that your last word?" asked the eldest brother. Something in his voice was surprisingly gentle. Harfleur got up to speak.

Mallard listened carefully to Nick's tale. When the youth had finished, he grunted. "Did the mercs leave quietly then?" he asked.

Nick nodded, noticing how Jem kept looking at her watch.

"We'd better be off, the tide is running," he said.

"Can't you stay for the vote?" asked Harfleur. "Both of you."

"Sorry, politics are not for me," said Mallard.

"Mother says everything is political," said Jem, looking at Fleur.

"Everything?" asked the tall girl, amazed at the idea.

"Everything IS political for your mother," said Mallard. "Make sure she doesn't get her hooks into you."

Before Jem could reply, three fishermen pushed their way past.

The unlucky creature didn't know it had been caught and was still fighting for its life. Jem marvelled at its translucent scales. It looked as if it had been moulded out of plastic rather than born swimming in a bitter ocean. The men cursed as they struggled to hold on to their thrashing see-through dragon. One of the fishermen lost his grip.

Jem stepped back, looking at the creature's lidless eye as rows of serrated teeth rose and fell like knives in a canning factory. This was ironic, thought Jem, as that was exactly where the fishermen were taking it. Nick sighed and pulled out his tazor. The display showed four green bars.

On the second zap, the monster let out a shriek and stopped thrashing about. The fishermen laughed in approval. Nick wondered what they would think back in London if they saw him wasting two precious tazor zaps on a runaway fish.

"That fish will feed 50 mouths," said Harfleur approvingly.

"Turn 50 stomachs more like," said Nick. "It stinks!"

"Its insides started to cook when you zapped it," said Mallard. "I had a beastfish steak for supper last week. It wasn't bad."

"You'll eat anything that's drowned in krill sauce," said Nick.

Jem maintained an impatient silence, refusing to engage.

"The seas have been rich with fish ever since you came and made the Stormfather turn again," said Harfleur, looking at Nick.

They crossed the slipway to where Mallard's boat was moored.

"We're pleased for you luv, really we are," said Mallard.

"It's probably the vibrations that are causing it," said Nick enthusiastically. "Big fish are drawn to low frequency sounds."

Harfleur gave Nick another admiring look.

"Not coming back to London with us then?" asked Mallard.

Nick avoided Jem's eyes as she stared at him sulkily.

"No," said Nick. "I promised I'd help here. There's a string of wind farms out past the island. We're going to try to fire them up."

THINK JEM! WE'LL ALL BE RICH AS SEA KINGS!

DO WHAT YOU LIKE.

Jem and Mallard got onto the boat. Mallard waved. Jem didn't.

"Safe sailing!" called Nick, annoyed that he couldn't think of any better words of parting. An old fisherman, who'd been watching, grinned a jagged grin. He held up a couple of fish.

"Caught two beauties on one hook have you lad?" he laughed.

"Can it, you worm!" snapped Harfleur.

Chapter 2: Ocean steal

Harfleur and Nick were searching for the second Stormfarmer – the giant wind turbine that was going to make them rich. Nick wasn't greedy by nature, but something a guy in the charging shack had told him had really hit home:

"We all worry about saving money. Well, the man who turns the power on - all he's gonna worry about is how to spend it."

The guy was right. Whoever controlled the wind turbine would be rich. Nick didn't see why it shouldn't be him. So he'd ridden his luck, deciding to cross to the second Stormfather in the winter rather than waiting for summer. It was risky going now when freak waves were not unknown. Nick's gamble had nearly paid off, but there had been a flaw in his calculations.

"I don't understand," moaned Nick. "We should still have a third of a tank of fuel left. I must have messed up somewhere."

Harfleur didn't do sympathy. Nearly every word she said was practical. There were words for girls like this, 'cold' was one of them. But that wasn't Fleur. Not deliberately, at any rate. Empathy just wasn't in her emotional vocabulary.

"We'll drop anchor here. I'll take the inflatable. That way, we won't waste fuel trying to moor," said Nick.

"Are you sure?" asked Fleur. "The sea is rough."

Sometimes when she spoke it seemed as if she cared about him. Or was she just weighing up the chances of him losing the inflatable and getting her involved in a risky rescue.

"We could return with more fuel?" she suggested.

"And look like a couple of jellies who can't navigate?" snapped Nick as he killed the engine. "Let down the anchor.."

Nick threw the rope back to Harfleur who caught it first time without even looking, despite the swell. A thin plastic hull stood between Nick and a quarter of a mile of freezing water. But he trusted the Series Three inflatable. The tough little boats were standard issue for the YPD, where Nick had done his training. As the waves edged the boat closer to the ladder, Nick decided to jump for it.

"I'll go first," he called over the noise of the motor.

5 metres below, something was stirring.

The engine's thrum had carried far down into the deep ocean. Curious, the beastfish had followed the unusual noise. As Nick's outstretched hand reached for the rusty ladder, he suddenly felt the boat tip and roll beneath his feet. For once, Nick was caught off guard. He was pitched into the freezing sea.

When it felt the sound of Nick thrashing around in the water, the beastfish didn't need a second invitation. It shot towards the sound like a spark from a tazor – a dispassionate death-bringer. Harfleur saw a shadow under the waves and raised her harpoon. Drawing back her arm, she put all of her weight into the throw.

The harpoon arrowed into the water. When it pierced the creature's mouth it released its deadly charge of electricity. Coils of steam rose from its gaping jaws.

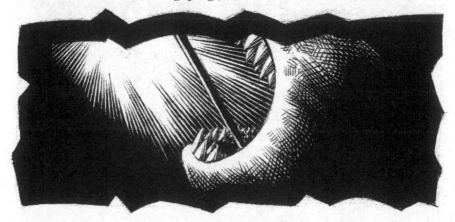

Nick hauled himself up the ladder, gasping from the cold. Meanwhile Harfleur had begun to haul on the rope and pull the creature out. It was a struggle. The thing weighed a ton.

Nick helped Fleur to drag the thing up onto the deck. The two of them wrenched it out like a rotten tooth. The monster's dead eye was already glassing over but it still seemed to have him in its sights. Its mouth tore at the air whilst spasms of sparks railed through its nervous system.

"Look!" cried Harfleur in excitement. "She was pregnant!"

Fleur ripped her harpoon out of the beast, opening its belly. A hundred wriggling beastfish babies spilled out onto the dock, their jaws already programmed to bite. Nick felt a brief flash of regret for the creature's doomed offspring, born alone in this hostile environment. Then he turned away in revulsion. The little beastfish had started eating their dead mother.

Chapter 3: Spark rush

NICK KICKED HARD BUT THE WEATHER STAINED DOOR REFUSED TO YIELD.

"Harfleur!" called Nick. "Get over here and help me!"

The pair had been searching the island for the last half hour but they still hadn't found what they were after. When pirates boarded a ship in ancient times, the first thing they went for was the map case. Likewise, Nick was after schematics, manuals – anything that could show how to get this giant wind turbine spinning again. Nick knew he was unlikely to make it work, but by coming here at least he was claiming it for Harfleur's people. The 'spark rush' had started.

Through force of habit, Nick went to wind up the radio before realising that it was battery powered. He called Fleur again. Then he gave the door another kick. At last, the area near the handle splintered into a forest of tiny spikes. Nick reached through the gap. As his chilled fingers searched for the lock, he heard a scuffing noise from the other side. Instinctively, he pulled his arm back nicking his wrist on a splinter. Crimson blood bloomed from the cut. Nick winced and cautiously moved his ear closer to the hole.

"Hello!" he called sheepishly. There was no answer.

"Nobody home," Nick muttered, annoyed to find that he was talking to himself. Flicking on the torch, he shone the amber beam through the hole. Moaning inwardly, he poked his hand through again and found the bolt. The door opened with a satisfying creak.

"Fleur!" he yelled. "Get up here."

A thin layer of white dust covered everything. It fell like snow in the torch beam. A column of light streamed down from above. As Nick's hand tightened on the tazor, he winced. Blood was trickling from the cut on his palm. His eyes were drawn to a figure slumped in a swivel chair. Slowly, the chair spun towards him. Nick noticed the uniform and the windmill logo. A poster on the wall read: 'Greenwheel: spinning a cleaner future.'

The figure struggled to its feet. Nick backed away, pointing the tazor at the figure. But it kept coming towards him.

"Stop!" ordered Nick. "Keep still or I'll light you up!"

The hands flailed at him again.

'Waaaattter!" moaned the figure.

"Okay!" gasped Nick, lowering the tazor and unhooking the water bottle from his belt. "Have some water. For Fill's sake! I almost fried you!"

At that moment, Harfleur crashed through the door, with a charged harpoon at the ready.

But the harpoon was already flying from Fleur's hand. Harfleur's people believed that every event in a person's life has been decided already, from a baby's first breath, to death's last rattle. There had been times when Nick thought that they might have a point. But this was not one of them. Nick could not believe what he'd just seen. Fleur had attacked the man without warning. Sometimes he thought he loved her but now he couldn't believe her coldness.

Nick's face was pale. As he stared in horror, he noticed that the guard's face was covered in a spider's web of fine lines.

There was an unusual expression on Fleur's face. Nick saw that she was anxious and upset – shocked even. But there was no guilt. Fleur ran from the room, killing the conversation. Nick had no alternative but to follow her. When the pair reached the jetty, they found that the ocean was boiling with beastfish. Nick winced at the site of his old enemies, now back in force.

"First zombie guards, now mutant fish!" he moaned.

Fleur was first down the ladder. As she was climbing down, Nick saw the seriousness of the situation.

The boat was taking some serious damage from the beastfish.

Nick turned instinctively when he heard a shout. The door of the guard house opened and a bearded figure stumbled out. He wore the same uniform as the other guard. Nick raised his tazor and checked the gauge. It was showing four bars out of five.

"Halt! Stand still and you will not be harmed," he warned.

Predictably, the stumbling figure did not stop.

"Easy Fleur!" cautioned Nick. "I can stun him..."

"Get back!" screamed Harfleur. "Get back or I'll send you through the Seventh Gate!"

But the bearded man didn't stop. He came stumbling on towards them. A series of low growling sounds were coming out of the man's mouth but it was impossible to make out what he was actually saying. He didn't sound friendy!

Nick gripped his tazor and hesitated. Even in these days of affordable electricity, he still had to think twice before firing a tazor.

Harleur had decided what to do. She pulled back her arm, ready to throw the spear.

Nick sighed and shoved Fleur off balance. This made it impossible for her to use the harpoon. Nick didn't like hitting people without a reason (or a direct order from a superior officer). Sighing, he stepped in and and threw a punch at the bearded man. The blow connected but the man kept on coming.

"Waaaaaaaaa!" he gasped. Nick threw a second punch and the man dropped to the deck.

Harfleur looked at Nick, open mouthed.

"You touched him!" she said in a horrified voice.

Nick couldn't understand Fleur's disapproval. She'd had no qualms about killing the guard in the tower. Why was she so upset about him punching the guard out now?

"I had to stop him," said Nick. "He was a threat."

Fleur twisted her harpoon to charge it with electricity.

Not for the first time, Nick had misunderstood her meaning.

Before Nick knew what was happening, Fleur brushed the harpoon against Nick's cheek. The weapon sparked and Nick fell to the deck.

Chapter 4: Missing

Nick woke up to the rush of white-noise, like a radio tuned off station.

The noise was everywhere. At first he mistook it for the sound of rushing water, then he thought it was his own imagination. Finally, he realised that it was the wind. Nick found himself at the bottom of the ladder where he'd fallen. He climbed up a rust stained ladder to an observation platform, where the guards had once looked out across the empty ocean through a toughened glass window.

"Fleur!" he called. But there was no answer. He became aware of a burning thirst and caught sight of his own reflection in the glass. Instinctively he put a finger to his cheek where a faint spider-web of fine lines had appeared.

"She's left me!" he said in disbelief.

Nick reached for the water bottle at his belt, but realised that it was missing. His mind was frazzled. He didn't recall that Fleur had warned him about offering water to the guards. Then he remembered that they had gallons of drinking water back on the boat.

As Nick climbed back down the ladder, his head was reeling. His fingers slipped off the steel rungs and he slid groundward.

Struggling to his feet he retraced his steps to the jetty. Nick noticed that he was finding it increasingly hard to walk in a straight line. He called out for Fleur again and again but his hope turned bitter with each unanswered shout.

At last Nick made it back to where he'd punched the bearded man. The place was deserted now. Nick scanned the area for anything that might contain water. Looking out over the expanse of steel grey ocean, Nick's heart sank. The inflatable and the launch were gone.

"Fleur!!!" he screamed.

Chapter 5: Tank

WHEN NICK CAME AROUND, EVERYTHING IN HIS LINE OF SIGHT WAS
SMEARED INTO A DARK AND DIRTY BLUR.

Nick became aware that he was submerged in salt water. The
temperature was low. In a panic, he spluttered out his last mouthful
of air. Had he just wasted his final breath? Cursing himself for not
being more careful, he kicked and wriggled, trying to free himself.

As the last bubbles of precious air leaked from his mouth,
numerous questions raced around his brain. His head felt brittle, like
an egg-shell. The next thing he felt was a tickling sensation near his
mouth. Then he became aware of the rubber tube, taped to his cheek.
Seizing it in his teeth Nick gratefully gulped in a mouthful of air, and
then another and another. Bewildered, he struggled to swim to the
surface, but something was weighing him down.

A familiar shape snaked into Nick's line of vision. Fear drifted through his body like smoke. The beastfish made a pass around the tank but it soon collided with the glass and doubled back. It was about a metre long, only a young specimen, but still armed with teeth like gutting knives. Worse still was its venom. Famously, the beastfish could eat you alive, and the only thing you'd know would be the puff of your blood in the water. The creature came towards him, its glassy eyes saw nothing but its body sensed his magnetic field. At first he thought it would pass by but it doubled back, coiling itself like a python and struck him on the neck. There was no pain, just a slight bump. He jerked away, twisting for his life.

The creature continued on its circuit until the front of the glass tank stopped its progress. Then it looped gracefully back on itself and returned for a second strike. Nick flexed every muscle trying to pull away from the beastfish. But it was useless. Before it could hit, Nick felt himself lifting up into the air. Slowly, he was being hauled out of the tank. Still struggling, he spat out the air tube and coughed.

Nick clutched the wound on his neck. The hooded figure produced a linen dressing and pressed it against the wound. A sweet scent filled the air but a stabbing needle of pain made Nick flinch and bite his lip.

"Ssssssshhhh!," repeated the figure in the hood.

The pain began to fade slightly.

"Who are you?" gasped Nick. "Where am I?"

The cloaked figure laughed. "Two fine questions. The first one is easy," and with a practiced swish she removed the veil from her face.

"River??!!" said Nick. "What are YOU doing here?"

River's eyes flashed. "Saving YOUR worthless hide, police boy," she answered.

Nick eyed the woman in the way that an injured stalk eyes a passing crocodile. The last time he'd met Jem's terrorist mother, she'd been ordering her daughter to leave him to die. Now she stood opposite him, her green eyes wide like opals.

"Why would you ever want to help me? I'm still a YPD," he muttered.

"Good point!" laughed River.

In a fluid movement she snaked out her hand and released the handle causing the chain to jerk down. Nick suppressed a cry as he dropped back into the tank.

AAAARRRGGHH!!

"Ooops!" said River as Nick let out a slow scream of terror.

A second pull on the lever stopped the chain from falling.

"Sorry," laughed River. "I couldn't resist it."

It took five minutes to extract Nick from the tank. As she unbound his hands, River explained her motives.

"I've got my reasons for helping you. I hear you've left the Youth Police. We have a soft spot for deserters – don't we sister?"

The hooded figure replied again with her customary: "Ssssshhhh!"

"Is that all she ever says?" asked Nick. "That could get really annoying."

SHE'S TAKEN A VOW OF SILENCE.

"They're healers. They believe that a silent life brings you closer to your heart." said River.

Nick considered this for a moment.

"They could be right," he said. "I wish you'd shut up."

The shssster replaced her veil. Nick smiled awkwardly, trying to ignore the disturbing image. Then he turned his attention back to Jem's mother.

"Who says I've left the YPD?" he asked flatly.

"My source says you've not made a single report for 3 months now. Your precious Mander must be worried. I expect London have got their best drones looking for you as we speak."

"What if I haven't quit the force?" asked Nick.

"You will," she said, reaching out to stroke his cheek.

DON'T TOUCH ME! I'M INFECTED!

YOU CANNOT HARM ME. I'M IMMUNE.

River smiled. "And you could be healed too..."

Nick touched the wound on his neck. The pain was fading.

"I'm sorry about the tank. Beastfish venom is the only thing that can arrest the sabat khat disease," continued River.

"'Sabut what?" asked Nick.

"You call it 'threadneedle'" she explained.

River offered him a bowl of soup. He drank it and winced.

When I became infected like you, I remembered a tale about a lost island of healers. It turned out to be this place."

"What is this place?" asked Nick.

"That depends.." answered River. "On whether you are for us or against us?"

Chapter 6: Shattered lens

THE VOYAGE BACK TO LONDON HADN'T BEEN PLAIN SAILING FOR JEM AND HER FATHER. After two weeks in a boat, Jem felt tight, like an overwound watch.

Mallard grunted and raised the teapot, ready to pour.

"I'll do my own," snapped Jem.

"You should see the look on your face sometimes. You look like you've lost a pearl and found a pebble," he said.

Jem put the teapot down but she didn't refill her mug. At first it had been okay spending some time with her father. However, the long days at sea had drained her of small talk. It wasn't for lack of trying, but the words dried up on her lips before she could get them out.

"It's not my business," began Mallard. "But if I were you I'd give Nick a break. He's 16 now. He can't be in the YPD forever. He's right about the wind farms – if they can start them spinning and generate electricity, the islanders will be set for the rest of their lives."

JUST THINK OF THE POWER!

I AM, IT'S TOO MUCH!

Jem had a point. Harfleur and the Islanders had been cut off for so long. They weren't used to the ways of the world. Mallard shrugged his shoulders in defeat.

The conversation stopped. Jem soaked herself in a bath of August silence. It was weird to be hearing true quiet once again, after months out in the tearing wind of the Stormfather Island. Jem's thoughts kept turning to Nick. She tried to fight it, but her eyes began to roll again in annoyance.

"Where is he now?" she wondered. Probably trying to impress Harfleur with his collection of difficult knots.

The boat moved up and then down on a passing swell.

"Waves are made purely by the power of the wind," thought Jem.

She imagined what it would feel like to be a wave. You'd be made of moving power and intent. You'd have a destination.

Mallard edged towards the figure in the doorway, trying to act like a man who wasn't holding a full teapot in his right hand.

The APD taught hand to hand combat at the academy. Their instructors claimed that after passing the course, any officer could go up against multiple knife wielding assailants. Mallard had only just scraped through the final exam, but armed with a pot full of freshly brewed tea, he was dangerous.

"Drop it!" snarled the intruder from behind the mask.

Mallard noted that the stranger was wearing an old fashioned diving suit with the sort of markings that used to be called futuristic before the Climate Upgrade. The suit was old but it was in pristine condition.

He was still wondering whether the stranger's neoprene suit was tea proof when a harpoon whizzed from the gun and connected with his right shoulder. The teapot exploded like a water bomb, drenching Mallard in scalding hot tea. Jem screamed and rushed over to try to help her stricken father.

"Dad! Are you OK?" called Jem in a panic, sprinting across to the doorway and carefully easing the metal barb that pinned her father by the cuff of his threadbare jacket.

"I'll live," winced Mallard through gritted teeth. "Not sure about my jacket."

"Pity!" sneered the intruder.

Jem fixed the stranger with one of her 'nuclear' stares.

"You're going to hand me that 'poon gun," she ordered.

River glared at Mallard. Mallard clutched his wounded shoulder and winced.

"You've gone too blooming far this time woman!" he roared.

"Shut up, it's only a scratch," replied River.

Mallard staggered towards the table in the centre of the cabin.

"Only a scratch?" he boomed. "You've shot a 'poon into my arm! You daft piece!"

River's eyes flashed back at him.

"Shut up you great Yorkshire pudding!'" she hissed.

Jem sighed. It was business as usual. This time she believed her mother. She reckoned River had meant to fire a warning shot into the cabin wall. Sadly, harpoon-guns are not accurate above water.

"What do you think will happen when the authorities in London find out that the islanders have their own power source?"

Jem shrugged. She hated the way her mum's voice got deeper when she got serious.

"Well Jem?" asked River. "Will your precious Mander let the islanders keep their power?"

Mallard had stopped nursing the hole in the cuff of his favourite jacket and now he was absent mindedly spooning multiple sugars into a cup. He didn't looked up as he began the counter argument.

"London will have to pay the Islanders good money for their electricity. They'll all be compensated," he explained in a calm voice.

COMPENSATED?
LIKE THE ABORIGINALS
IN PRE-FLOOD AUSTRALIA?
OR THE MAORIS? OR THE
CHEROKEE?

Mallard tried to respond but River hadn't finished her list.

"... or the villagers who lived in the gas fields of Cumbria…"

Jem looked up. She was used to hearing about the terrble crimes committed against the unfortunate people on this list. She'd heard it many times before. All except the folks of the gas fields of Cumbria. They were a new addition.

"The Cumbrians? What happened to them?" she asked.

"They got fracked," snapped River.

"What are you talking about mother?" asked Jem in a weary voice.

Now it was River's turn to let out a sigh.

"The gas companies came and sucked Cumbria dry. It's the same story all through history Jem. It happens whenever the strong meet the weak…"

River wagged an accusing finger at Mallard.

"It's happened a thousand times before. And now your father and his APD friends are going to stand by and let it all happen again.

"Why?" asked Jem, turning to her father.

"Because that's what policemen do," said River.

River leaned forward and smiled conspiratorially.

"The APD is a corrupt police force. They serve their own leaders, not the people," she said.

"The YPD just as bad," said Mallard.

River shook her head.

"The APD are even worse than the Youth Police Jem. People get better at lying as they get older."

"But why the pirate role play? Why didn't you just…"

"Drift over? For a cup of tea and a chat?" snapped River, finishing Jem's sentence in the way that only a mother can. "I thought about it. But I couldn't run the risk that Skipton over there would run back to his APD bosses and blab."

"Skipton?!!!" scoffed Jem, amazed to hear this new nickname for her father.

"Learn a lesson that I learned on my mother's knee… never trust the powers that be," explained River.

"How did you find us?" snapped Jem. "The ocean is immense."

"Ask your ex-boyfriend," said River. "He's good with maps."

"Well you can drop your weapon," winced Mallard, clutching his wounded shoulder. "I'm not returning to London to make a report…"

"Don't buy it Jem!" growled River. "Pleased don't let him sell you a lie."

"I'm not selling anyone anything," he said flatly. "I'm retiring." This answer was the last thing that Jem expected to hear from her father. She looked at him in amazement. An awkard silence spread through the cabin. The boat moved up and down without warning, rocked by a passing wave. No one noticed it. Finally, River exploded with laughter.

"Him? Retire?" she scoffed. "They'll sail him out of his police station in an undersinker's launch."

Mallard shook his head sullenly and repeated the information that he was quitting the APD for good. Jem didn't understand why. The law was his life, but she knew from his eyes that he was completely serious.

"Why?" demanded Jem.

"Because… I can't do it anymore," he answered in a rather apologetic tone.

River rounded on the wounded APD officer.

"What's the matter? Grown a conscience have we? Or is it a touch of the man-pox?" she laughed.

"I'm serious," said Mallard.

Jem gasped. Bur her mother laughed as she stepped out of the shadows, flicking her hair back from her cheek.

Horrified, Jem stared in disbelief. She could see a tell-tale web of criss-cross lines spreading from a patch high on her mother's cheek.

Chapter 7: M25

YOU'RE INFECTIOUS! IF YOU REALLY CARED ABOUT JEM YOU'D LEAVE US ALONE.

River didn't respond, she just turned to Jem.

"Is that what YOU want Jem?" she asked.

Jem looked her mother in the eyes. They were as clear and blue as the Thames. She wondered what went on behind those lenses.

"Mother,' she began. "Why are you REALLY here?"

The concerned expression left River's face. At first it was clear but then it got weaker and weaker, like a fading radio signal.

"I'm here to shut your father's mouth," she said matter of factly. "Before he tells the whole of London about the 'electric island' where the streets are lined with lights."

Jem nodded. Her mother had issues with empathy. Was this her version of honesty?

Before Mallard could defend himself they crashed to a halt.

"Bloomin' eck!!" cried Mallard.

"You've crashed the boat – you great oaf!" screamed River.

"Mother...," began Jem in the peacemaker voice she reserved for family occasions like this.

"Sorry Jem. I'm an emotional wreck," snapped River.

"Come on!" cried Mallard.

Jem followed her father, picking her way through a mess of

broken plates and stubbing her toe on the smashed teapot. Mallard winced as he struggled up the ladder with the others in tow. At last he made it to the wheelhouse. There, he stood like a Yorkshire Priam, peering out into the morning mists. The sea was as flat as an ironing board. Chilly trickles of evaporating mist ran down Jem's cheek. Reaching the rail and looking out, Jem saw that her boat was caught in a ring of rusting military hardware.

Jem studied the string of grey objects that dwarfed her boat. On closer examination she saw that they were spiked with sensors.

"Can't you navigate?" snarled River. "You've steered us straight into the M25!!!"

"Pardon me," said Mallard. "But I was too busy being hi-jacked and harpooned to notice that we've drifted off course."

The M25 minefield had got its nickname because it formed a huge ring around London, along roughly the same route as its namesake, an ancient motorway.

Jem stuck out her hand to touch one of the grey metal spikes.

Then she had second thoughts and drew her arm back. River took a pair of field glasses from a pocket and scanned the horizon.

"I'm sorry my dear but if you can't tie up a jetski properly, you deserve to get it exploded," tutted Mallard

"These mines look old – pre-flood maybe?" observed Jem, tactfully changing the subject.

"Get my ski back you Yorkshire pudding!" ordered River.

"No chance," said Mallard. "The mines are old. But they still have a lot of boom in them."

River leaned towards him, preparing her next verbal volley. Something along the lines of Mallard having a lot of cake in him. But before she could get her words out, Jem asked a question.

"Why is the light on that one flashing?"

River snapped into survival mode.

"Where's the life raft?"

"We don't have life rafts," answered Mallard gruffly.

River's face went white. Jem had never seen her mother this angry before. It was an epic anger, as wide as the march skies.

"No life rafts!" screamed River. "And YOU dare to lecture me about my daughter's safety?"

"She's my daughter too," corrected Mallard.

"How would you know?" hissed River.

"I know my own child," replied Mallard.

"Only because you had her blood tested," spat River.

Mallard fought the urge to let the argument esculate.

"We don't have life rafts...." he explained calmly.

WE HAVE ZEPPLINS INSTEAD.

"For Fill's sake!" said River. "You've got to be joking!"

Jem sighed. Her parents could go on like this for hours. Then she noticed the worried look on her father's face.

"What's the matter?" asked Jem.

"We've only got two zeppelins!" moaned Mallard. "They're designed to carry one person each."

"You're the heaviest dad," said Jem. "You go in one and mum and I will go in the other."

"Absolutely not!" barked Mallard. "That woman is infected. You are not going anywhere with her!"

Jem sighed and rolled her eyes skywards.

"How much do you weigh dad?" she asked.

"I'm not sure love... 90kg maybe," he replied hesitating.

"And the rest!" laughed River. "That Yorkshire pudding hasn't seen his feet for many a year."

"Be quiet woman!" snarled Mallard. "Let me think this through."

"There's no time for this," said Jem. "I'm going with mother."

Shaking her head, Jem climbed into the first zeppelin.

"Move it!" said River, clipping herself into the harness behind Jem. "We're in a minefield, remember?"

Mallard clambered into the other harness.

"Meet me at Canary Dwarf," said Mallard.

Jem stared blankly back at her father.

"You know – the little wharf by the old tower," said Mallard. "We'll rendezvous there tomorrow at sunrise."

He went to pull the launch cord but something made him stop. Jem recognised the look on her father's face – it was fear.

"But Jem..." he began. "Do you know how dangerous threadneedle..."

"Later!" said Jem pulling the launch cord for him.

With an explosive thwock, the bolts shot away and the zeppelin rose upwards into the grey sky. Mallard called out a final warning.

But Mallard's voice was lost in the wind. Jem peered up at the departing balloon, fighting back the tears.

"What did he say?" she asked.

"Oh nothing I expect," said River. "It was probably just some pithy phrase. He saves up witty comments for crisis situations like this."

Jem glared at her mother. Her sullen expression showed she blamed her for the situation they were now in.

"Don't look at me" said River. "If your father hadn't eaten all the pies, we wouldn't be in this mess."

Before Jem could reply, River pulled the launch cord. Four explosive bolts shot away and the second zeppelin rose magestically from the deck.

Instinctively, Jem hugged her mother. Then, remembering her father's warning about the infection risk, she let go and held the rail instead.

The zeppelin was rising silently upwards into a palace of grey clouds.

Jem looked down at ocean. She could see a string of battleship grey pearls sweeping westwards in a gentle arc. Each pearl was deadly. River had control of the steering, and the zeppelin turned slowly, following the direction of Mallard's craft.

Jem was still thinking about what to say when there was a distant explosion from far below.

Chapter 8: Dead zeppelin

MUTTERING A STREAM OF OLD FASHIONED CURSES, MALLARD PULLED ON HIS CRASH HELMET AND BEGAN TO STUDY THE MAP. His zeppelin was travelling faster than the other one because it was lighter. When he came out of the cloud bank, Jem's craft was nowhere to be seen. Flying blind was exhausting – the hours dragged. Through breaks in the cloud he caught the occasional glimpse of black sky flecked with silver stars.

Mallard flipped the throttle open and the engine responded. The craft climbed until it was cruising above cloud level. The moonlight bounced off the tops of a blanket of marshmallow clouds. Mallard smiled, the moonlight really was silvery, like in the old songs. Maintaining his height for long would waste fuel, so he let the zeppelin slip back into the cloud bank. A sudden jolt shook him awake. The dome of St Paul's was coming up fast.

At last he had a point of reference. Steering the zeppelin to the east, he headed towards the rendezvous. Mallard's harness was heated with wires, but the cold had got into the bones of his feet and hands. Forty minutes later, he could make out the familiar sight of the floating market beneath him. His watch said 8:15am – he tapped the luminous dial. Like most of Mallard's treasured possessions, it was a relic. Had its battery finally given up the ghost? The walkways and pontoons of Greenwich were empty. The market was deserted. All of a sudden, a stinging blow hit Mallard on the helmet.

"Cheeky little nerks!" shouted Mallard, shaking his fist at the youths. Then he patted his crash helmet.

"If Goliath had had one of these on his head he'd have given young David a proper thrashing," he muttered.

Mallard decided to set the zeppelin down in the market. Aiming at a large pontoon, he landed with a thud. Impressed with his skill, he rose triumphantly to his feet. Then he fell over. The cold in his legs had made his legs so numb that it was impossible to stand. Mallard took his crash helmet off. Then he checked his watch again. It read 8:19am.

By now the market traders should be setting up their stalls, but there were no lanterns lit, no steaming bowls of krill noodles for sale. As he sat trying to rub some heat into his frozen limbs, he glanced around. Mallard's eyes were drawn to a sign.

At that moment Mallard heard the sound of boots crashing down the path. The next voice he heard was the excited shout of a child.

"There's another one!" cried the voice.

"When do we get our finder's fee?" asked a second voice.

"When we've safeguarded him and not before," came the muffled reply.

20 metres above the struggle, Jem peered down at the two guards attacking the figure. Even from that distance she could see that the guards were wearing some kind of bio hazard suits.

Jem grabbed the steering rope and the zeppelin swung back in a wide arc, losing height as it went.

She could see that far below, the guards had put restraints onto Mallard and were dragging him towards their boat. It was an APD Keep boat with a large steel cage. It looked pretty brutal.

She thought she could could hear Mallard's protests as the steel door slammed shut. Or was she imagining it? She looked at her mother with pleading eyes.

Jem felt her mother's hand encircling hers and gently pulling on the steering rope. The zeppelin rose gracefully through the air, to a height where they could easily track the progress of the cage boat. They noticed the other craft on the river veering away from the cage boat as if it were a great white shark.

"How bad is this disease mother?" gasped Jem. "You said you were infectious..."

"No I didn't!" laughed River. "I never said that. Your father just assumed as usual."

"But... your face," began Jem.

"I caught it. But I've been vaccinated. I'm immune now but I'll never lose these scars. It's a good thing that the tribal look is back."

"I thought threadneedle was fatal," said Jem. "Dad told me that adults are the carriers."

"Wrong again!" laughed River. "It used to be a death sentence, but some friends of mine have been working on the cure."

"Are they sure they can cure it?" asked Jem

"Let's say they're quietly confident," said River.

Jem felt the zeppelin turn into the wind as her mother pulled the rope to the left and the craft responded. To Jem's horror, the craft began to move away from the tower.

"Take us back!" pleaded Jem.

Jem could not understand the coldness in her mother. At some level, she thought it must be an act but she had shot a harpoon at Mallard and now she was about to leave him to his fate.

"I'm not abandoning him!" sobbed Jem.

"Use your eyes Jemima," said River.

Jem followed her mother's outstretched arm until she saw a grey plastic object the size of a dinner plate.

"YPD Drone," said her mother.

Jem didn't get it. Since the Agreement, all drones had been outlawed, along with projectile firearms. Were the YPD flying machines again? It was against everything that they stood for.

"I can't believe it," muttered Jem.

"I can," said River. "But the question is, what is it doing out here?"

When River dropped the zeppelin down out of the cloud bank, the reason for the drone's presence was clear. A huge convoy of boats was heading south east – away from London.

"A convoy," said Jem.

"They're evacuating London," said River.

Chapter 9: Evacuation

ON THE FLAGSHIP, THE MANDER ADJUSTED HIS MASK.

Giving the order to evacuate London had been hard but it had come down to a simple choice. Stay put and rule a plague torn city, or sail off in search of limitless power. It hadn't been difficult to get the youth to agree to his plan once he'd agreed to take a few of the healthy adults as well. A wise Greek had once said: "If you give me a fulcrum, I can move the world."

Fear of the 'needle' was a great lever.

Chapter 10: Hesaid

MALLARD HAD BEEN IN THE CAPTURE BOAT FOR AN HOUR BEFORE IT ARRIVED AT ITS DESTINATION.

"Safeguarding?" muttered Mallard under his breath. He didn't like the sound of that, it had YPD written all over it.

The guards avoided contact with the prisoners as the cage boat cut its motor and glided serenely up to the reddening jetty.

Mallard stood up in the cage, gripping the bars. The guards on the walls were armed with riot batons and harpoon guns. Mallard sat back down and began to whistle a half forgotten tune.

One of the guards was speaking on his radio, but it died in the middle of the conversation. Cursing, the man flipped out a lever and began to wind frantically, to recharge the radio. Mallard studied this scene. It was the first time he'd seen anyone winding a radio for months. It seemed like stone age behavior but electricity was still in short supply here in London.

At last the cage door sprung open and they were escorted up the wooden steps. The new intake consisted of 5 cases, including one irate Yorkshireman. When the steel gates opened, the guards backed away and retreated back onto their boat, as a jostling crowd of prisoners pushed forward. Mallard eyed the crowd suspiciously.

"Welcome to Safeguarding!" said a short man in a white coat.

"I heard him," said Mallard calmly, "but I don't have any water."

The smile died on the giant's face as he looked at his red hatted master for direction. An image flashed into Mallard's mind, of a circus ringmaster leading a trained bear.

"Sorry," said Mallard, his palms outstretched. "I've got nothing to share."

The bear stalked towards Mallard and grabbed him by the throat. It felt like being caught in a steel trap.

A jeering crowd formed around them, as jeering crowds do. The giant's great paw tightened around Mallard's throat. In an inner pocket, Mallard had hidden a water pouch. Now he was wondering if it had been a wise decision to conceal it. He was just about to give it up when a female voice called:

"Let him go Hesaid! He doesn't have any water. The Safeguarders search everyone before they come in here."

Grumbling, the giant dropped Mallard and shuffled off.

"Don't mind Hesaid," laughed the woman. "He's harmless enough when you get to know him."

"He-said?" asked Mallard. "That's an unusual name."

"He-said get water, he said punch his face!" growled the women, impersonating the giant. "Hesaid just repeats the last thing that anyone's said to him. I guess it gives him something to talk about."

"There's a few people like that back at the yard," said Mallard.

Chapter 11: On the level

JEM HEARD THE MOTOR ON THE ZEPPELIN SPLUTTER. The fuel gauge needle had gone to empty over a minute ago, it was time to come down. It had taken hours to track the cage boat. The disc of the sun was dipping below the edge of the world by the time she spotted it. The river was deserted, and the YPD cage boat was unmistakable. She'd tracked its movements till it had come to the Column – the tallest building from old London. Two hundred metres of steel and mirrored glass wasn't enough of a fashion statement, so the architect had decided to stick Nelson's column on top of the whole thing. Only the top stack was visible above the waterline. One day, the river Thames would welcome it back with watery arms. But not yet. For now the greening giant loomed over the city from the western fence to the floating market.

Jem felt the rush of the wind as the zeppelin swooped towards the building. She willed the little zeppelin forward.

"This is suicide," thought Jem as she headed towards the glass wall. This close, she could see where patches of green algae had formed on the windows. Some of the windows were broken, maybe she'd put a few more out. The wind suddenly dipped. This close to the side of the building, the winds were unpredictable. Jem looked down at the landing point she'd selected, on the second level below the old column. But even as she had this in sight, the wind freshened again and the zeppelin lurched downwards. Jem's heart raced. The buzzing had stopped. With the motor cut, the mission had failed. Even if she could get into the Column, she had no way to fly her father out with a dead zeppelin. The glass wall flashed past her. In a panic, Jem looked for ways to arrest her fall. She was descending faster now – still many metres up. Time slowed as Jem fell into the darkness. There was a ripping noise as the harness jerked her about like a puppet in a badly performed puppet show.

Peering upwards into the night, Jem saw the problem. The shell of the zeppelin had got snagged on something. Now she was dangling in mid air. Craning her neck Jem saw what had trapped the blimp. It was a window cleaning cradle positioned half way up the side of the tower.

The height of the Column would have made her gasp, if the cold wind hadn't already stolen her breath.

Jem counted to three to steady her nerves and uncoupled the harness rope. Looking down was a bad idea, but in fact there was nothing to see, only the sea of darkness below her.

Heaving herself back up her own rope, she swung wildly, trying to make it to the window cleaning platform. The cold metal rail felt good in her hand. Swinging herself in, she collapsed in a heap. The place smelt like the inside of a birds' nest. Jem was still picking dirty seagull feathers out of her hair when her radio squawked into life.

Jem struggled to her feet and gazed down. Far below, a welcoming orange light shone in the darkness.

A yellow sign said: "Taxi." Then it winked out.

About ten minutes later, Jem was sitting in the passenger seat, dripping all over her mother's leather uphostery.

"A water taxi Mother?" moaned Jem in frustration. "I said we needed a fast boat."

River shrugged and steered the taxi away from the building. The taxi's illegal bio-diesel motor chugged away merrily.

"Where are we headed?" asked Jem. But her mother didn't answer.

WHERE ARE WE GOING, MOTHER?

WE AREN'T GOING ANYWHERE, MY DEAR.

"What do you mean?" asked Jem, with tears in her eyes.

"Sorry," said River. "I'm afraid that we've got to split up."

"But dad!" sobbed Jem. "We've got to help him!"

"That foolish man deserves everything he gets," snapped River. "Belive me, if he drops dead of the threadneedle this morning, it wouldn't be a day too soon.."

Jem knew her parents had problems but this was a new low.

YOU HELP HIM IF YOU WANT. I'VE GOT TO FOLLOW THAT CONVOY.

I CAN'T BUST HIM OUT ALONE. I NEED HELP!

River sighed and handed Jem a thin leather bag.

"Take this," she said. You have friends on Stormfather island," she said. "I have a boat that will get you there. It's the best I can do."

Chapter 12: Water

THE GUARD COUGHED UNDER HIS MASK AS HE WOUND UP HIS RADIO.

It was the only thing they wanted: water. It seemed cruel but the rules were that on no account could you give the threadies water. Even a few sips could set them off. The guard would not have believed it if he hadn't seen it with his own eyes.

At last the green light flickered back on and the guard stopped winding. The radio crackled into life.

"Three more hours," said a voice. "Three more hours and you'll be on the evacuation boat."

"Three hours," said his partner. "We might live through this shift yet eh?"

Mallard sat on a plastic bench out of the way from the main prisoners. The woman who'd helped him with the big unfriendly giant shuffled past. Her face was red and blotchy.

Something in the lady's eyes reminded him of his mother, now long gone. Mallard put his hand into his pocket and found the fluid pack. Sighing, he passed the plastic envelope to the lady.

"Sip it slowly love!" said Mallard under his breath. "We need to make it last."

"What do you think you're doing?" cried an outraged voice.

Mallard turned on this man.

"She's weak. She needs it."

The kindly expression slid off Mallard's face. As he watched the woman sip the water, he saw the tell-tale spider's webs of threaded veins spread across her face. The speed of the change was shocking.

Chapter 13: Goodnight

HARFLEUR TOOK THE CANDLE FROM THE BOX. The inside of the container was sealed against the wind. It was a solemn place – a place of remembrance. She had been here twice in her life. Each time to mark the death of a parent. It was a place that nobody wanted to go, but dread had turned to peace over the years. Fleur thought of Nick, lit the candle and placed it with the others.

69

When the ancient rhyme of remembrance had been said, Harfleur shut the door. The wind tore through her clothing as she made her way up the stone steps towards the meeting hall. It wasn't difficult to find, its lights were blazing in the evening gloom.

Lights make you feel warmer, thought Fleur, even if it was cold outside. If she had looked back at the container, Fleur could have seen the glow from Nick's candle streaming in through the crack in the door. But that door would always be closed now, and Fleur wasn't one for looking back.

At the door Fleur was greeted by Caan, who was checking for weapons. The meeting hall was packed.

"Any visitors today?" asked Fleur.

Caan nodded and smiled a grim smile. By 'visitors', she knew he meant mercs. The three freelancers had promised that they would be back for the new moon with another offer. They looked like they meant business. Fleur's face fell when she saw a familiar figure approaching.

The news stunned Jem. It took her breath away. It was so unexpected. She'd borrowed River's boat and arrived on the island to find help for her father. She'd almost forgotten about Nick and Fleur and their mission to the second Stormfather. The sea is always dangerous – but not for Nick. Nobody could handle a boat like Nick.

Jem felt sick with rage. She rounded on Harfleur with tears streaming down her face and glared up at her tall rival.

Lost to us?" she spat. "What does that mean?"

Caan stepped between the two women, and placed his hand on Jem's shoulder.

"It's serious," he whispered. "Your friend caught the sickness. I'm afraid he is lost to us."

"Where is he?" demanded Jem. "Take me to him."

Harfleur stood silent as the grave.

"He is not on our island," said Caan. "He can never return."

"Listen Caan..." said Jem in a cold voice. "He may be lost to your people, but you've got to help me find him."

Caan's snatched a tazor from his belt and powered it up. He pointed the gun but not at Jem. Three figures had appeared in the doorway.

Jem stepped aside as Caan stepped towards the intruders. Two of them pointed tazors at Caan.

"Here's our invitations," he said.

"Half a bar of power," said Caan. "You won't take many prisoners with that."

Harfleur stepped forward and placed herself between Caan and the tazor. She looked down at the Merc as a seahawk might look down on a baby seal.

"Leave now!" she said. "No one here is selling their share."

"Nobody wants to sell," said Harfleur.

"I might," said Jem.

Jem's hand went to the card on the chain around her neck. Jem unclipped it so they could get a better look.

When they'd first arrived on the island, it had been ruled by a mad man in a mask. Jem, her father and Nick had changed that. They had been rewarded with 'shares' as a token of thanks.

"It's the real thing," said Jem. "Ask Harfleur."

Harfleur's eyes went to Jem's. She wanted to speak, convince Jem not to sell her share. But she had closed the door on Nick today, perhaps it was best if Jem followed him.

"It's a share to one three hundredth of the island's power."

"Three HUNDRED charges?" gasped the merc.

"More, than that," she said. "This gives you a three hundreth of the island's power. For as long as the wind keeps blowing."

"Your price?" he asked.

"What's your name?" asked Jem, extending her hand.

"I'm Hass," replied the tall merc. "This is my brother Sreek."

Jem nodded. Then she pointed at the third merc.

"Who's the big guy?" she asked.

"That's Bump," said Sreek. "He's our bro too. He's not talking right now. He and Hass had a fight this morning..."

"Great," said Jem, rolling her eyes. "Very professional."

Sreek smiled. Bump said nothing.

"You were saying... Your price?" asked Hass.

"Have you heard of a building called the Column," asked Jem.

The tall merc nodded.

"My father is being held there," said Jem.

"Free him from the Column. That's my price. But it's dangerous. Are you prepared to take that risk?" added Jem.

Hass looked towards the town's bright lights with hungry eyes.

Chapter 14: Full blown

MALLARD WINCED AS THE SAFEGUARDERS WENT IN TO PACIFY THE WOMAN HE HAD TRIED TO HELP. He couldn't bear to watch.

The giant called Hesaid stepped towards the guard, but the safeguarder was ready with his stun club. Mallard heard the baton crack onto Hesaid's chest. The big man fell to his knees.

"Stay down or I'll zap you!" roared the safeguarder.

But the giant's eye had been caught by something he'd spotted on the dirty floor. It was the pupa of a moth.

The guards took the woman away. Mallard went back to his bench. A women was sitting in the place where he had sat before.

"When's feeding time round here?" he asked.

"It's nearly checking time," she said. "They'll check us first, and if we're clear they'll give us our ration packs."

"Roll on checking time," said Mallard.

There was no need to ask what the safeguarders were checking for. Mallard studied his own hands. They were red and puffy from the lack of fluids, but there was no sign of the tell-tale threads.

Ten mintes later Mallard stood in the square with the rest of the inmates assembled in rows. They'd come of their own accord, the guards hadn't needed to persuade them. Thirst had done the job for them.

A buzzer sounded, the iron gates slowly opened and a team of safeguarders in bio-suits came in. The guards ran their sniffer wands up and down the bodies of the assembled prisoners. If they were infected, the light on the wand changed from green to red.

"I'm clear right?" said a woman.

"Sorry love," said the guard. "It's just gone red."

"No! No! It's green! I'm clear!"

The woman collapsed in a heap at Mallard's feet. The other prisoners moved aside but Mallard instinctively helped her up.

"Don't touch her!" said a prisoner. "It spreads by contact."

The guard gave Mallard a sweep but the light stayed green. Mallard noted the guard's number. It was 106.

"Sorry 106 but it looks like I'm clear!" he said.

"Don't think for a moment that I'm liking this!" said the guard. "Two more days and we'll be out of this rat-hole!"

Chapter 15: The key

JEM LOADED HER STUFF ONTO THE BOAT, THEN SHE STUDIED THE FACES OF HER HIRED HELP. She'd never hired a fishing boat before. Hiring a team of mercenaries was a new experience. Before they could leave, the mercs wanted to charge up all of their equipment.

WE'LL NEED THAT CARD OF YOURS, LADY.

Jem thought that the three mercs didn't look much like brothers. Hass was tall with a long equine face and a thin moustache. Sreek was about half Hass's height. Bump was more than 'heavily built' – he looked like he had been assembled in a shipyard. Five hours later, they were on their way.

"Hass..." began Jem as the boat pulled slowly out of the harbour. "There's something you should know."

Hass glanced back towards the lights of the town.

"London is infected with the disease they call threadneedle," she said. "Have you heard of it?"

"Who hasn't?" replied Hass slowly.

"The good people of this island do not believe in helping the sick," said Jem. They think that the strong should abandon the weak. But this trip's dangerous. Are you prepared to take the risk?"

"For that share of yours, it's worth any risk," Hass said.

Jem scowled at the merc. She didn't like the way that this was going. Had that been the plan? To play the girl along until she was alone on the boat and then take the key card by force?

"It's a legitimate question," said Hass. "If we rescue your father but lose you..." he began.

Jem held up the card up.

"Let's get one thing straight," said Jem. "If I go, this card goes with me. Understood?"

"Understood," nodded Hass, but Jem wasn't convinced.

Hass hit the starter, gunned the throttle and the boat's illegal V8 engine roared into life.

Chapter 16: Chrysalis

MALLARD COULDN'T STAND IT — THE GIANT HAD BEEN STARING INTO HIS CUPPED HANDS FOR HOURS. He got up from his bench and slowly walked over to the big guy.

"What's that Hesaid?" began Mallard.

It was risky engaging with the giant. But every now and again Mallard liked to do things that were a bad idea.

"That's not a worm," said the young woman. "It's a chrysalis." Mallard shot a glance at her.

"She means that there's a butterfly inside," he began. "When caterpillars turn into butterflies, first they turn into one of those things. It's called a chrysalis." said Mallard.

"It's not a butterfly, it's a moth," said the giant, still staring at his hands. "He's coming out soon."

Chapter 17: Looking glass

THE BOAT ROSE AND FELL AS IT POWERED THROUGH THE RISING SWELL.

Jem pulled out the bag that her mother had given her and examined the thin round tablet. It was grey in colour, made of plastic and lighter than she'd imagined. The thing that grabbed her attention was the glass, it wasn't shiny, it was dull. Running her hand along the side, Jem's finger stopped on a round indentation. She pushed the button and held it in for three seconds, just as her mother had told her. Jem felt her heartbeat quicken as the dull glass exploded into a storm of lights. She almost dropped the box in surprise. Pulsing colours filled the glass circle.

At every level, Jem knew that this was forbidden. This was the world that her mother moved in, a world where there was nothing illegal about staring into a screen.

81

Chapter 18: Lose control

MALLARD WAS STOOD IN LINE AGAIN, THINKING ABOUT HIS NEXT RATION PACK.

"What's the delay?" asked the man next to him. "They've got us locked in this tank like a fish in a farm."

Mallard looked down the line of prisoners. The safeguarders had stopped in front of the giant called Hesaid.

"Scan him again, just in case!" ordered the captain.

Mallard noticed that the riot baton was shaking in the safeguarder's gloved hand. The guard was spooked.

Chapter 19: Three sisters

THE NOVELTY OF THE SCREEN WAS WEARING OFF.
Firing up the device now seemed as normal as winding up the kettle and yet people had killed and died for technology like this. Jem had used the device to plot their course until the red symbol stopped flashing and they'd reached the navigation beacon. Ahead of them was what looked like an abandoned ship – the sort of thing that pirates and powerjackers used as a decoy. It certainly looked the part with rust and a thick coating of grime.

"Ok, we're here, now what?" asked the tank.

"We wait!" said Jem nervously.

Her mother hadn't told her much. Her exact words were: "If you're thinking of saving the Yorkshire pudding, go to these co-ordinates first."

"What are we waiting for?" asked Sreek.

"Mother?" called Jem, as the boat drew nearer. A pale mist was streaming out from the cove but the sea was dead calm. It was a grey morning, still half night. The only sound was the slop slop slop of the oar blades as they bit eagerly into the water.

"Hello!" called Jem again.

There was no answer from the mystery ship. If it wasn't for the row of red guide lights on the prow, Jem would have sworn this vessel had sailed out of a dream. At last the boat drew closer. Jem got a better look at the three figures.

"Long robes," thought Jem. "Why doesn't that surprise me?"

As the boat drew up the figure raised her palm in greeting. Jem hailed her back and threw them a rope. The boat pulled alongside and one of the figures stepped aboard.

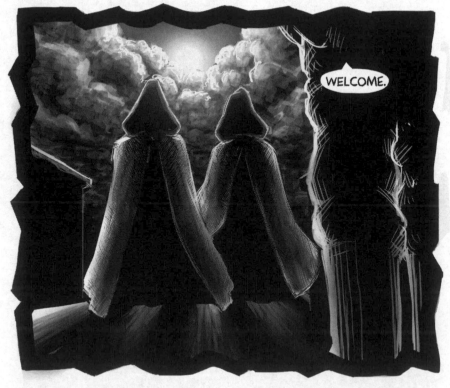

The robed figure handed Jem a tube and indicated that she should open it. Inside there was a note:

This sister knows how to cure rats.
P.S.
She won't speak, so don't waste your breath.

"Is she legitimate?" asked Sreek, stepping back from the figure.

"What's your name lady?" asked Bump.

The figure in the robes didn't answer his question.

"Don't waste your time," said Sreek. "She won't fall for your sweet talk."

Jem gave Sreek a withering look.

"She's taken a vow of silence," she said. "That's enough of a sacrifice without you hassling her from here to London."

"Are you sure about this?" asked Hass. "Passengers on this mission will only slow us down."

Jem nodded. "I'm sure."

Hass shrugged his impressive shoulders.

"You're the 'Mander," he replied.

Chapter 20: Safeguarding

THE SAFEGUARDER WAS RELIEVED. The call had just come through that the evacuation was going ahead. In the yard, the crowd of prisoners had thinned out. Lines of bio bags were heaped in a pile in the courtyard. But even with these numbers of cases left, bailing out of here wasn't going to be easy.

The YPD captain had a point. There were only thirty staff working in the Column. It had never been designed as a prison. In order to evacuate from the landing stage, his safeguarding team would have to walk right through the main courtyard where the prisoners were waiting.

Mallard studied the scene. The guards were taking their time leaving. The C.O. in charge waited for his team to assemble.

"Hurry!" he said quietly. But the words came out in a stage whisper. Mallard was not the only one to notice what was happening. Soon the yard was swarming with angry inmates.

"Safeguarders!" yelled the C.O. "Withdraw immediately!"

"Hey screws!" called a tall prisoner. "Safeguard this!"

A wooden bench was hurled through the air. It crashed into the guard, felling him like a pine tree. A row of inmates rushed at the line of safeguarders, who answered their surge with a hard rain of batons. Those prisoners who were too sick to move were caught in the rush for the gate. Seeing a chance for freedom, Mallard tried to work his way towards the front. But the APD officer didn't have the heart to do the elbow work required to break through this seething human stew. The steel gates slammed shut.

"Evacuation complete!" announced the team leader.

Chapter 21: Towers

THE SUN SLID LAZILY DOWN THE SIDE OF THE BUILDING. Darkness would follow it home. Jem's screen had guided her safely through the M25 minefield and into the heart of the city. But she'd arrived to find London empty. Birds sang to each other and rats roamed the walkways at will. Jem didn't know it, but the last ship of the evacuation had already sailed. There was nothing in sight, not even a drone in the sky.

Jem cast her mind back to school. She used to love it when the storycaster came to visit. One of her favourite tales was called 'The Towers of London'.

Once before our time, (the story went), there was a greedy Knight and a crafty Fox who held a competition to build towers out of glass and steel. Soon, a hundred towers rose on London's skyline. They spread like weeds and grew like sunflowers, each one taller than the last, the storycaster had said.

And every time the Knight built a tower, the Fox would build a taller one. And if the Knight's tower was tall, then the Fox's tower had to be taller. This went on, month after month, year after year, until London lived in the shadow of these glass giants.

These towers were tall, but they were hollow. No one lived or worked inside. These giants stood empty. For no one wanted to move into an empty tower. Besides, the rents were as high as the lead-coloured sky. One day, a poor old woman asked the Knight:

"Why are you building towers when the people of London have no roofs over their heads?"

"To keep up with the Fox, of course!" answered the Knight.

But, as the historyteller explained, the REAL answer was that the greedy Knight owned the builders and the glass factory and the steel company. And building the towers kept his firms in business and earned him money. And as long as the Fox was building too, the lenders kept lending money to build more towers, and selling shares in the empty giants. And that was why the Towers of London stood for years and years until there was no crack left in the London skyline wide enough for even one more glass tower.

The Climate Event at the end of the Phone Age had put a stop to this. But the last tower that the had Knight built was special – on top of it, he'd put the old statue of London's greatest hero.

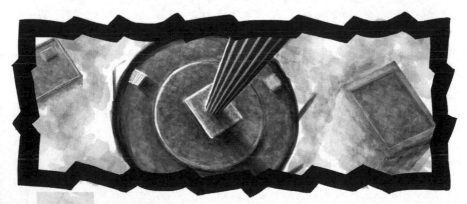

Nelson had always fought for London. His statue was old and powerful. The Mayor wept as he sold it, but the city was bankrupt. So he had to sell it to the Knight, who crowned his tallest tower with it. And the legend said: that if ever London was in mortal danger. Its hero would come out of the statue at the top of the tower and come to the aid of the city.

Jem twiddled her hair. The mercs were right, this looked too easy. Where were all the YPD Krew boats and drones? The Column stood in the middle of a millpond. All they had to do was knock on the door and enter.

Jem shuddered. What if her father had already been taken? Was he still alive? The uncertainty was hollowing her out, like a worm devouring an apple from the inside.

Feeling an unexpected hand touching her shoulder, Jem turned and saw a hooded figure. Beneath the dark hood she could make out the woman's fair hair and slate grey eyes.

Jem winced and turned away. Close up, she could see the scars where the ssshter's lips had been permenently closed in the silence ritual.

Why had the woman put herself through the harrowing ordeal? To willingly seal her own mouth, prevent herself from sharing her thoughts and ideas? Had this been born from a wish to cut herself off from the world? Was it an act of rebellion, or submission? An image swam into Jem's mind. She put her finger to her own lips and shuddered. Had silence been the woman's choice? Or had she been pressured into it?

Jem gazed up at the tower. Its mirrored windows rose skywards, level after glassy level. The ssshter's eyes were steady and certain. Her lips were sealed but her soul still had its windows intact. She took her hand away from Jem's shoulder. One touch had been enough to show Jem how she felt.

Hass interrupted the moment.

"Hey sister!" he called. "Time you were leaving. Meet us at the poor door."

There was an awkward silence.

"Sorry! I keep forgetting. Nod if you understand," said Hass.

The sister nodded.

"You've lost me bro," said Sreek. "What's the 'poor door'?"

"In the old days these towers had more than one entrance," explained Hass. "The rich went in the front, and the poor people had their own door."

"For real?" asked Sreek.

Hass nodded.

"How about our silent sister?" asked Sreek. "Is she coming?"

"She's a shsssster, not a ninja," said Hass.

The four watched as the boat edged away from the entry dock and disappeared into the distance. The sun was slowly dipping as the sound of its motor faded. When the ssshter's boat was gone, the windless river was as flat as a table.

"What happened to your boots?" demanded Hass.

Bump shrugged. "I left 'em in the boat," he said nervously.

Jem muttered under her breath as she squeezed her body into her suit. It was a struggle to slide into it. She shot Bump a fierce glare. He seemed to find the process amusing.

"Stop stretching your suit. It'll start reacting," advised Sreek.

"What's this thing made of?" Jem moaned.

"Liquid armour," said Hass. "It's filled with a kind of stab proof custard."

The calm was shattered as a harsh voice pierced the silence.

"Safeguarded area. Withdraw immediately!" it crackled. A bell chimed out at the end of the announcement.

Bump's eyes lit up and he flashed a smile.

"There goes the Big Bell?" he said.

"Big Ben you mean," said Hass. "You great clock-wit!"

"Nah," said Bump. "It's Big Bell! London is famous for it."

"He's legitimate!" laughed Sreek. "It's called Big Bell"

"Enough," sighed Hass, his whisper as loud as a shout in the still air.

They moved towards the steel gate at the foot of the tower. In the dying light, the Thames was blacker than the river Styx. As they drew nearer, Jem lost track of the scale of the building. The glass-windowed giant bestrode the river and the market.

Jem gazed up at the tower. Its mirrored glass reflected the dark water. But areas of the glass were encrusted with lichen so the image was crazed with lines. Jem shuddered at the sight of her reflection. The voice crackled out its warning again.

"It was probably just an old sample," said Hass matter-of-factly.

"A Safeguarded area?" said Sreek.

"You never told us it was a plague tower," moaned Sreek.

"I told him," said Jem looking at Hass. Bump shook his head. Jem pulled out her share card and thrust it into the merc's face.

Bump and Sreek seemed content to go on. Meanwhile, Hass was examining the gateway. He pointed at a sensor panel at the side of the grand entrance.

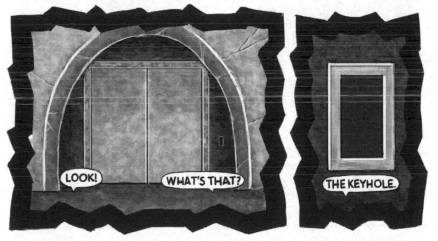

Bump stepped towards the door and pressed his hand against the glass.

"I had a job cleaning windows once," he said. He threw back his bull neck and craned up at the brooding glass cliff. "It took ages."

"Use a sponge next time," said Sreek.

"Leave the safeguarded area," announced the voice again.

The four suited figures stood on a jetty at the base of the immense building. Whilst the others watched the shadows playing on the glass, Jem and Hass examined the gate. Jem ran her fingers over the panel. Unclipping the key card from her necklace, she pressed it against a sensor. A red light flashed briefly, but then it winked out.

"What now Miss?" asked Sreek.

"Hmmm," said Jem. "This is the part where an ancient motor was meant to come back to life and slide the door open."

Before the words were out of her mouth, a metallic whirr broke the silence.

"Legitimate!" said Sreek. "We're in!"

But the great gate stayed firmly shut.

Jem gasped. The building seemed to be sprouting like a fairytale beanstalk, rising up before her eyes.

"Get ready," said Hass. "We're sinking!"

In a panic, Jem realised that the wooden boards beneath her feet were slipping down into the dark Thames. The jetty was retracting and sinking fast. Jem felt the cold spreading through her as the water covered her boots and rose towards her waist.

Hass raised the harpoon gun and shaped to fire but then he had second thoughts and lowered it.

"What's the matter?" asked Jem, clinging on to Hass.

"Don't touch me," snapped Hass. "Keep still!"

Jem trod water silently for what seemed like an age until the whirring stopped and the jetty was fully submerged.

Jem gulped in a couple of short breaths and tried to stop herself shaking. Her liquid armour suit offered precious little protection against the chill of the Thames.

Hass raised the 'Poon gun and took aim. At that moment, the brown water around his knees began to boil like a soup-kitchen kettle.

But before Hass could fire the harpoon gun, the water around him bubbled red, like a crimson volcano.

"What's that red stuff in the water?" cried Bump, instintively clutching at Hass.

"Get off me!" ordered Hass, pushing the big merc away and raising the harpoon gun. "I've only got one shot at this."

"Bubbles!" laughed Sreek, but the laugh died on his lips when he saw what Bump had been referring to. The water was incarnadined with streaks of crimson and rusty red.

"Blood," Sreek gasped. But his cry was drowned out by the noise of the raging flood.

Chapter 22: Wet hen

MALLARD CRAWLED OUT OF THE WASTE SILO AND COUGHED. If age and experience had taught him anything, it was that if you have to hide in a drain pipe to save your life, then you go and hide in a drain pipe. Shame didn't not come into it. He was crying, but they were only pepper gas tears. Fighting the urge to wipe his eyes, he slowly moved the handkerchief away from his mouth. The yard was quiet. The battle for the gate was over, the safeguarders had gone. The rioters had payed a heavy price. The safeguarding team had called in a drone strike.

Mallard didn't ask any questions. The girl's eyes told her story.

"I'm Leem," said the girl. What's your name?"

"Mallard," said the DCI, trying to stop his voice cracking. As the girl stepped towards him, a light in the ceiling activated and lit up her face.

"You're not dangerous," smiled Leem, taking his hand. "Where are we going?"

Mallard sighed. "Up," he replied.."We're looking for a way up."

Leem smiled. "I know where there's a ladder," she said. "I'll show you."

The girl led Mallard though the rubble towards the far corner of the chamber. When she found the place, she looked back and a tear tracked down her dusty cheek. Mallard put his arm around her and turned her away from the scene.

"Are you angry?" she asked.

"Yes love," said Mallard. "I'm madder than a wet hen."

Chapter 23: Treadwater

RUST RED BUBBLES SPREAD THROUGH THE SWIRLING WATER AS JEM STUDIED THE FACES OF THE MERCS. Sreek and Bump were clinging to each other. Hass was treading water. He still had the harpoon pistol. A thin climbing line was attached to the harpoon and coiled over his right shoulder. Jem became aware of the dark shapes snaking through the water around her. She balled up her fist and began to smash at them. But Sreek grabbed her wrist with his gloved hand. He nearly wrenched her arm from its socket. Jem winced, amazed at the terrible power in his thin arm.

Sreek raised a gloved hand and thrust it into the whirl of red bubbles. Jem clung on desperately treading water, wriggling like a maggot on a hook.

"The rats are part of the building's defences," explained Hass, swiping a rat off his brother's shoulder. "The designers put a lot of bio-security into old stacks like this."

"Why rats?" gasped Jem, clinging to Sreek.

"Rats are scary," said Sreek, holding one of the creatures in his gloved hand. It thrashed its scaly tail and bared its yellow teeth.

"They're cheaper than guard dogs too," he added. "And if you forget to feed them, they'll eat each other."

Sreek made as if to kiss the rat whilst tightening his grip. He had the rodent by the throat.

"That's a strong grip," said Jem. "Have you been working out?"

"Servo gloves," said Hass. "Got micro-motors in the joints."

"Good thing we're suited up, or we'd all be rat meat by now," said Sreek. "Ain't that right Bump?"

But the merc didn't answer. Jem looked at the creature in Sreek's gloved hand. It had curled itself up into a sleek ball.

Jem starred at the writhing ball of brown fur in disgust. Then Bump began to thrash around, kicking and screaming.

"Keep still!" ordered Hass but the big merc wasn't taking orders.

Without the protection of his liquid armour boots, Bump's feet were vunerable. Meanwhile, a rat was scaling the dock wall.

It was making its way towards Sreek's face but he caught it in his gloved hand. The water was boiling. Writhing bodies scrambled on top of each other and shapes moved under the water.

"Rats can't stay underwater for that long," said Jem. "How come they don't drown?" asked Jem.

"All part of the building's bio defences," said Hass. "They've been modified."

He twisted a rat's neck to reveal an unusual flap of skin.

"Gills on rats?" said Jem. "What were they thinking of?"

"They did some crazy hacks in the days before the Upgrade," said Hass. "Dolphin torpedos, exploding bees..."

"Exploding bees?" said Sreek. "What's the point of that bro?"

"Swarm weaponry," said Hass. "Didn't you go to the Pastkeeper's Palace? You should take an interest in history."

"Sure I went to the Palace," said Sreek, casually smashing another rat on the head with his LA glove. "But I was only interested in the robots."

"You and the rest of London," said Hass. Then Bump screamed.

Hass spotted a plastic bag which had floated to the surface. He held it up towards the struggling figure of Bump.

"Listen to me," said Hass. "The red bubbles are coming from a blood sack. They release a blood sack at the same time that they release the rats. It gets them all riled up."

Bump nodded.

Hass aimed the harpoon pistol at a point high above them.

"What are you waiting for?" yelled Sreek, swatting a rat with his left hand. "It's a big enough building bro! Even you can't miss it."

"I'm aiming for the top windows," snapped Hass. "Now shut up and stop thrashing around!"

At that moment a rat sprang snarling towards Jem.

GET IT OFF ME!

Sreek grabbed the rat. It could not escape the vice like grip of his liquid armour gloves. Jem didn't feel sorry for it.

Ignoring this chaos, Hass aimed at the window and fired. The line snaked out and there was a crash as the dart found its target.

"Who's first up?" asked Hass.

"Me!" moaned Bump.

"Ladies first," said Sreek. "Sorry bro but she's the lightest."

Hass pulled the line to check it would hold and then clipped it to a carabiner on Jem's belt. It was a struggle, in the end he had to take his gloves off to screw the clip into place.

Jem pulled on the line, and tried to haul herself up the taut rope, but it was hopeless. Her boots slipped on the smooth glass.

"Do you think you'll still be afloat by the time she makes it up there without your gloves?" spat Hass.

"Lend her YOURS then," suggested Sreek selfishly.

Hass cursed and pointed his pistol at Sreek.

"Give her the gloves now!" he ordered.

Muttering under his breath, Sreek took the LA gloves off and handed them to Jem.

"Thanks bro," said Hass. "Was that really so difficult?"

Jem put on the gloves and gripped the rope. There was a quiet whirr as she made a fist. She felt an uncanny strength in her hands.

"There's no need to grip so hard," advised Hass. "The fingers have servo motors, they'll stay locked until you let go."

Jem understood why Sreek had wanted to hold onto the Liquid Armour gloves. Having vice-like grips on both hands made climbing easy. Trying not to look down, Jem began to inch her way up the side of the glass giant. Craning her neck upwards, she followed the rope until it disappeared against the dark tower.

Ever since she was a little girl, tall buildings had held a weird fascination for Jem. She would sneak out after curfew, slip under the barriers and scale the tips of submereged skyscrapers. Climbing was a buzz but when she reached the top something disturbing always happened. A nagging voice from her subconscious insisted that she should throw herself off into the rushing wind. Jem was bothered that her own mind could throw up such a destructive suggestion. Jem imagined the thoughts packed together inside her brain, like bubbles in a bath – bubbles of memory with a few bubbles of madness inside an otherwise logical thinking machine.

Fighting the impulse to look down, Jem moved one gloved hand over the other, until finally, she could see the cracked window where the thin line of rope stopped. After what seemed like an age, she drew level with a window and swung her feet in hard.

The ancient glass was eggshell brittle. Soon she was pulling herself in through the remains of the broken pane. In the still night air, Jem could hear bickering voices far below her.

"Why didn't you give her YOUR gloves?" demanded Sreek. "It's a legitimate question."

"Your hands are the same size as hers," sighed Hass. "If we are going to accomplish this task, you need to stop questioning me. The Evil Empire wasn't built on backchat. That's what my grandfather used to say."

Jem felt a sudden shake on the line. Instinctively, she gripped the line with her right hand. Far below there was a sudden splash.

"What was that?" she called.

"The rats!" called Hass. "They're climbing up behind you."

It was the bewildering height, rather than the rats, that held the fear for Jem. Thinking about it left her sick and dizzy.

"Put the gloves in the bag," ordered Hass. "Clip them to the line and lower them back down."

Jem did as the merc instructed. A shout from Sreek told her

that the parcel had been delivered. Sreek went to clip the line to his belt, but Bump stopped him.

"Let him go next," said Hass. "Anything to shut him up."

Grumbling, Sreek passed the rope to Bump, who clipped himself on. With impressive upper body strength, he hauled himself out of the water single-handedly. Then he let out a high pitched squeal, kicking at the rats that had clamped themselves to his shoes.

Chapter 24: Limelight

MALLARD AND LEEM HAD CLIMBED THE 'LADDER', BUT THEY STILL HADN'T FOUND ANY WATER. Mallard's throat burned like fire coals. He could tell that the girl was weakening too. Only water could save them, but that thought had been thought before.

"Which way now?" asked Leem.

"Up, of course," replied Mallard with a smile.

Mallard's grin looked forced at the best of times. He wasn't sure how much the girl had worked out about their worsening situation. They stood in a long corridor on what must have been the mezzanine level. Mallard spotted the fire exit sign and led her towards the stairwell. But something stopped her in her tracks.

Mallard mopped furiously at his brow with his handkerchief. It had seen a lot of action over the last 72 hours. He sighed and turned his attention towards the girl. She could only be six or seven years old but she had a wise head on her shoulders.

"Who are the childminders?" asked Mallard. "Why are we hiding from them?"

Leem explained with a seriousness that only six-year-olds can do.

"We're hiding. I play this game with mummy."

Mallard wondered if this was some kind of imaginary friend type scenario. Or was the idea of a 'game' just Leem's way of coping with this frightening situation. He scanned the corridors and stairwells for signs of life but there was nothing but dust.

"It's no fun hiding when there are no seekers," said Mallard. He reached out to take the girl's hand but then he shuddered as he remembered the risk of infection. Withdrawing his hand slowly, he tried to talk her into moving.

Chapter 25: Sound and fury

JEM AND THE THREE MERCS STOOD BY THE BROKEN WINDOW AS HASS UNPACKED THE EQUIPMENT. Bump had a rat bite on the foot where the rats had gnawed through his shoe. For once, he wasn't complaining. No one spoke. Hass got out the first aid kit.

Jem's torch swept the room, lighting up the walls with its cold beam. The hotel was more shabby than chic. The expensive marble on the walls had lost its Italian glow. Now it was peeling off, like enamel from a rotting tooth. Motioning to the others to follow, Jem approached the door in the far corner. The calm was broken by a rasping noise. Hass reached to his belt and produced a tazor and a face mask. The others followed his lead.

Jem let out a sigh and edged towards the door. She gripped the handle and yanked it open.

"Die!" yelled Bump, firing indiscriminately into the seething mass of rats. The creatures rushed over each other in a panic.

"Stop killing them" called Jem. "They can't harm us now."
Here on solid ground, Jem felt strangely sorry for the creatures, cast adrift with only each other for food.

"You bit MY leg, and for that YOU must die!" cried Bump, in a monomaniacal rage. His tazor screeched and the rats squealed. Hass stepped over to where his brother was blasting.

"You're wasting power bro," warned Hass. "And you're making enough noise to wake a Kraken."

The mercs were a strange crew, thought Jem. Bump was good at the sound and fury side of things, Hass did all the signifying.

"Put your tazors on stun," suggested Sreek.

"Thank you," said Jem, surprised at his compassion.

"You'll still kill 'em but we'll save electricity."

Chapter 26: Childminders

Mallard was a poor liar. Of course he recognised the sound of tazor fire when he heard it. It was impossible to tell how far away the shots were being fired. Was it safeguarders? Or something worse? There was no option but to keep climbing. It was a vain hope, but Mallard knew that buildings like this had restaurants on the top floor. In the pre-flood days, the great and the good sipped drinks at sundown whilst they enjoyed London's skyline. The pair had climbed staircase after staircase in search of water. Mallard was consumed with thirst now. When he saw the restaurant sign, his stomach went tight.

A shameful thought swam shark-like into Mallard's mind. If it was a choice between the girl and water, Leem would have to wait.

She followed him to the steel door, but no further. Mallard lowered his voice to a whisper.

"Listen Leem. I'm really thirsty," he explained. "I need to find water. Perhaps there'll be some in here."

The child looked up at him with steely eyes, then she turned her gaze towards the swing doors in front of her.

"Not there!" she said. "Please!"

Mallard sighed. He had a clear recollection of how determined Jem had been at this age. "She's not a follower, she's a leader." That's what Jem's teacher had said. 'Stubborn' was the word that Mallard would have used but most parents didn't want to hear that.

"All right," said Mallard, fighting to keep his voice positive. "Let's play a game."

"I'm not playing," said Leem, stubbornly. Mallard ignored her and carried on speaking, in the way that parents do.

"You run and hide," he said. " I'll close my eyes and count to 10." Leem nodded. Mallard gripped the door handle, ready to open it, and began to count...

1,2,3,4,5,6,7,8,9...

"Ten!" whispered Mallard, pushing the door gently open. His eyes instinctivly scanned the corners for threats. The place seemed empty. Mallard's throat was burning. A uniformed figure stirred in the shadows at the back of the room. He woke to the noise of the opening door and staggered to his feet. Mallard saw the tell-tale craze of threaded veins across his face. With a slow deliberate walk, the figure shuffled towards Mallard.

The figure was a guard. He still held his radio, but the winder had snapped off. He'd called and called but his buddies in the safeguarding team had abandoned him.

Mallard span around at the sound of the croaking voice. Now he had two threats to deal with: the guard and a woman. From this distance, he could see the threads and lines, like finely inked tatoos that had bloomed across the women's hands and face. She was now in the full grip of the disease and mad with thirst. Muttering something deep in her throat, she advanced towards him. She was joined by the Safeguarder, who still held his broken radio in his clenched fist. Mallard sidestepped her and smashed his way back through the door. Then he heard Leem's voice calling.

Mallard moved in the direction of Leem's voice, trying not to panic. His head was spinning like a turbine. He racked his brain for places where the girl could be hiding. Crashing through the next door, he found himself in a reception area.

"Leem?" he called again, but this time there was no answer. Peering through a porthole into the main dining area, he saw that he was near the very top of the tower. To his left and right the restaurant wall swept in a pleasing curve of glass. They'd taken pride in their designs before the Climate Upgrade, Mallard thought.

Mallard put his hand on the door – ready to open it – when a child's voice broke the silence.

But Leem's warning came too late. Mallard was already pushing on the heavy oak door.

Mallard and Leem rushed through the crowded dinning room towards a sign that read 'viewing gallery.' The crowd were in different states of threadneedled distress. The possibility of water seemed to flick a switch within them, engaging their curiosity and driving them to investigate. Picking the girl up and lifting her onto his shoulders, Mallard rushed towards the sign.

Here at the top of the tower, guests could climb a final ladder that led up to the centre piece of the building. At the base of the famous statue of Nelson, which had been transplanted from its ancient home in Trafalgar Square, diners could peer out on the winking lights of London. They'd look down upon old Father Thames as it snaked its way through the ancient city, older than the hills and as thin as a shoelace.

"I bet you're a good climber" said Mallard putting Leem down and pointing up at the famous statue. "Can you climb up there?"

"It's too high," replied Leem.

"Nonsense!" said Mallard, fighting the impulse to pick her up, for fear of passing on the infection.

"It's too high,' repeated Leem accusingly.

Outside, sleet was falling in long cold daggers. Warm tears ran down Mallard's face as he carefully helped the girl up onto the plinth below the great column. He wondered whether the city's greatest hero would be offended. Mallard knew his history. Old Nelson was a fighter, he'd probably approve of this glorious last stand.

Searching around for weapons, Mallard let out an exasperated gasp. Under a piece of wooden board, he spotted a piece of scaffolding pipe. The metal felt cold in his feverish hand. Mallard tried out a few practice swings, sending the pipe tearing through the air with a satisfying whizz. Then he put the weapon down. Battering sick members of the public with a metal pipe was not his idea of good police work.

Angry shouts came from behind the door. Mallard shuddered as the door swung forward. Then a noise from his left made him turn rapidly and pick up the pipe again.

A metal ball cannoned into the small merc's arm. He let out a shriek and dropped the tazor, clutching at his wrist. Amazed, Sreek looked up towards the statue and snarled a curse.

A second missile shot from Leem's catapult, with such force that it embedded itself in the chest piece of the big merc's suit.

Bump picked the missile out of his suit. It was a metal marble, the size of a pigeon's egg. Scowling, he drew a knife from his belt and turned towards Mallard.

"Excuse my daughter," said Mallard, backing away. "I got her that catapult for her birthday and now I'm regretting it. Say 'sorry' to the armed man Leem."

Mallard stared wide-eyed in amazement. "Er, helllo luv!" he gasped. Mallard felt his legs weakening, and he slumped down onto the oily floor. "Sorry about the daughter thing, it's a long story."

Jem rushed towards him but he backed away, protesting.

"Stay back luv, I'm in a bad way."

Jem took a single pace forward but stopped in her tracks.

"Leem! You can come down now," called Mallard. "This is my daughter Jemima. Don't copy her. She's not a good role model."

"What do you mean?" moaned Jem.

"She hangs around dangerous young men with tazors," coughed Mallard.

"Says the man with the steel pipe in his hand," said Jem.

This touching reunion was cut short by the muffled thud of the glass door rocking on its hinges. The door shook but it didn't give way. Jem peered at the seething crowd of threadneedled faces on the other side of the toughened glass.

"Water, water!" they demanded.

"What now?" asked Mallard, struggling to his feet.

An unknown object hammered against the door. Jem stepped back. It was followed by a succession of increasingly heavy objects.

Mallard raised the metal pipe.

"Nice thought dad!" said Jem. "But that's graphine glass. There's no way anything is getting through that without power tools."

Through the smoked glass, Jem took in a sea of desperate faces. A wooden pole smashed against the glass, making no impression on the barrier. Seconds later a sledge hammer connected and a crack spread through the glass.

"Sledgehammers?" moaned Jem in exasperation. "Do people carry tools around them in case of apocalyptic scenarios like this?"

Mallard shrugged his shoulders.

"As we know," he said. "That door won't hold them for long."

"Stand back" said Bump, powering up his tazor and striding towards the door with a smile spreading across his broad face.

"You actually might want to step back dad," said Jem. "I've seen him shoot that thing."

The sledgehammer connected with merc's gloved hand as he threw the door open. But the liquid armour took the sting out of the hammering blow.

The man with the sledgehammer dropped like a felled oak as blue sparks railed through his body. Steam rose from the hand that had held the hammer. The shouting crowd stalled for a moment, stuttering like a fuel-starved engine. Seizing his chance, Hass slammed the door shut again.

As Mallard staggered back from the door, Jem moved to support her ailing father.

Chapter 27: Shining path

JEM LOOKED AT HER FATHER AND TRIED NOT TO CRY.

"Leaving you behind is not in the plan sir," said Hass as he threw his pack to Bump. Bump failed to catch it and stood gawping at the bag in bewilderment.

"Break out the descent gear," Hass sighed.

Opening the pack, Sreek uncoiled a rope and threw it up to Leem, who was still sitting on the ledge at the base of the statue.

"Wrap the rope round and throw it back," he demanded.

"Do what?" asked Leem in a puzzled voice.

"Wrap the rope around the base of the statue," explained Mallard patiently.

"Nicely done Leem," said Mallard encouragingly. When Jem saw the little girl's face light up, she gave him one of her withering looks. This wide eyed girl might be cute but she didn't like the idea of an adopted sister. Especially not one with a catapult.

Mallard didn't touch the gloves, instead he turned to Jem.

"I'll never make it down by rope,' he said.

"You won't need to," said Jem, "we're going down in the maintenance cradle."

An expression of relief came to Mallard's face. He coaxed Leem down from her perch and put the gloves on. Hass tested the rope, leant back and then confidently abseiled off the ledge.

At that moment, they heard noises. The crowd on the other side of the door were regrouping. A heavy object slammed into the broken door. Leem looked nervously back up towards her hiding place on the ledge as Bump powered up his tazor.

Leem looked at the gun and stepped back from the merc. Jem let out a long sigh.

An uncomfortably long silence was finally broken by the reassuring whir of a motor. Far below them, the maintenance cradle began to rise.

"Sorry about the wait!" called Hass from the cradle. "I thought the motor was dead, but I got it going."

"Jump in! It's faster," suggested Jem.

"Use the rope bro!" yelled Sreek. "This thing will never take your weight..."

Before he could finish, the glass door finally gave way.

The barrel of the tazor sparked blue again and again. The blasts stunned the first oncomer and he began to convulse. He tottered and finally dropped, filling the void with his scream.

Leem cowered in terror. Mallard sat slumped in the corner of the cradle, with his hands over his mouth. At last, the cradle began to move. They went down about five meters but then to Jem's horror the cradle stopped descending and moved sideways along the face of the building.

"Sideways?" sighed Jem. "Why aren't we going down?"

"Sorry," moaned Hass, this thing has a life of its own."

"We need to descend," said Jem. "Unless you can fly."

Hass worked the joystick but the motor had ground to a halt. Sreek and Bump threw a stream of insults at their brother.

"Stop shouting!" said Hass. "Let me work this out."

At last, the motor came to life, but to Jem's horror, the cradle began to rise back up towards the baying crowd.

Hass pawed at the controls in desperation but nothing he tried could stop the cradle's ascent. As it crawled back up the side of the building, the crowd began to roar in excitement.

"Quick!" cried Jem. "Before they're within jumping distance."

But the crowd were already moving. An athletic woman lowered herself from the ledge. Jem could see the soles of her shoes.

Jem tapped Hass on the shoulder and studied the controls. She tried pushing the joystick to the left and right but it didn't respond.

"I told you, it's broken," said Hass in a dead voice.

Startled by a cry from above, Jem looked up. A threadneedled form had climbed down the cable, clinging on with uncanny strength. When Bump squeezed the trigger, nothing happened.

"No bars! It's dead bro!" he moaned, shaking the dead gun.

"It's working!" said Bump triumphantly. "It's rebooting."
Jem grabbed the tazor from Bump's shaking hand.

"What are you doing?" cried Bump as the threadneedled woman
advanced, scrabbling at the rail. 'Shoot!"

Jem fired the tazor again. A blast of blue sparks raked across
the control panel. The maintenance cradle stopped ascending and
jerked to a sudden halt. Then it began to glide slowly downwards.

"What happened?" asked Hass. "How do you manage that?"

"Emergency cut out," said Jem. "When the system fails the
cradle descends. Like how elevators go to the ground floor."

"Hey bro," said Bump. "We've got still company!!!"

"Water!" moaned the figure at the rail, clinging on with
threadneedled fingers. The mercs backed away. Mallard looked on,
as if the word 'water' was consuming him.

"There's water down there," said Sreek, "Look!"
The woman looked down, spell bound by the sight of the river

below as it loomed larger and larger.

"No!" cried Jem in horror. "Don't jump!"

But the hangers on didn't wait until the cradle had come to a halt. The lure of the river Thames was too strong for them. They threw themselves willingly into its watery embrace. Two loud splashes carried through the night air. Peering our across the dark river, Jem located the spot where the jumpers had landed. She hadn't given up on the idea of trying to help them. But river was boiling, the floating forms of the woman and the man were swamped by a sea of rats.

Jem looked at the merc's face and wondered what it must be like to inhabit a world where other people were just obstacles to be overcome, like pieces in a board game.

She stared out towards the ripples. Two innocent people had just died in front of her eyes. Saving them from their sickness hadn't been within Jem's power. But at least she'd found her father.

"Sorry bro!" said Bump. "My tazor's really dead this time"

Jem checked on Mallard. He was sat hunched at the back of the maintenance cradle.

"Are you OK dad?" she asked, trying not to sound petrified.

"Never been better luv,' answered Mallard in a low croak. "What happens now?"

Jem flicked on her torch and swept the beam across the surface of the black river.

"Can I have a go?" asked Leem.

As a child Jem had dreamed of owning a torch this powerful. The idea of a torch with its own batteries, that you didn't need to wind up, was every child's dream.

Jem hesitated, and then passed the light to the child who giggled in excitement. Wherever the torch beam hit the water, a cloud of iridescent points of lights blinked back at them.

"Death jellies," moaned Hass. "They've come in on the tide."

"Don't sweat it!" said Bump punching Sreek hard on the arm. The liquid armour suit cushioned this unprovoked attack. Sreek didn't feel a thing. "We're suited up? Remember?"

"They're not," sighed Jem, pointing at Mallard and Leem.

"Look!" said Leem.

Jem rubbed her weary eyes in disbelief. A familiar figure in a long flowing robe was coming slowly towards her out of the swirling mist. Jem and the others watched the approaching figure in silence, spellbound by what they were witnessing. The ssshter's feet seemed to be gliding across the surface of the Thames. Jem blinked. The ssshter was walking on water.

"How is she doing THAT!?" asked Jem.

"It's a blooming miracle!" declared Mallard in delight.

The shssshter came towards them, stepping calmly over the tox-ic jellyfish as if they were daisies in a field. Jem blinked again. However she looked at it, the shssster was actually walking on water. Sreek and Bump looked on in awe.

"Is that legitimate?" asked Sreek.

"It must be some kind of power," muttered Hass.

"She's a mystic, for sure," whispered Bump in amazement, pressing his hand over his heart. "She's walking... on the river!"

Jem smiled like an adult watching the children's faces at a storycaster's show. She'd spotted a thin line of fluorescence snaking back behind where the shssshter had been walking.

"Look!" whispered Hass in a low voice, as if he was afraid that if he spoke out it would break the spell and send the tiny figure crashing into the dark river. "Look at the water under her feet."

"What's she doing?" asked Sreek.

"Saving our skins," declared Jem with a smile.

Under the surface of the water, Jem could just make out a narrow pathway, made of a thin transparent material. The path was submerged under the slate grey water. It was practically invisible until the woman's feet touched it. At the touch of her steps the water fled from her toes like iron filings repelled by a powerful magnet. As she approached, the mercs saw through the trick and began to nod and laugh.

"Hey!! That's cheating!" said Bump.

Hass scratched his chin and peered out into the sleet. The night was getting stormy, arrows of rain freezing in mid air before they ripped into the choppy surface of the water. The hooded women edged ever closer, and a full moon slipped out from under a spectral veil of clouds.

"Where did she get hold of a shining path device?" asked Hass.

"Why ask me?" said Jem. "I dunno. The same place got your liquid armour."

Chapter 28: Bottle

BACK ON THE SHSSSTER'S BOAT, MALLARD WAS IN A BAD WAY.

The walk back to the shssshter's boat had been straightforward enough. The shining path hugged the edge of the building, providing a safe track to the 'poor door' where the boat was moored. When they'd missed the rendezvous she'd come to investigate. Or so Jem guessed, for the woman's lips were sealed.

Jem boarded the boat and let out a quiet sigh of relief. It felt good to be safe below deck. It felt good to get out of the liquid armour suit too. Meanwhile, the shssshter was busying herself in the galley. A few minutes later she emerged and handed out steaming mugs of clear soup to all of the party, except Mallard.

"Where's Dad's soup?" asked Jem, forgetting that the woman in the long robe could not answer her. The shssshter met Jem's eyes and shook her head sadly. She walked forward and placed a comforting hand on Mallard's shoulder. Mallard nodded.

Jem looked at the woman with renewed respect. She wasn't afraid of threadneedle. That was more than you could say for the mercs. Hass and the others were hiding at the other end of the cabin, as far from her father as possible. Even the girl Leem now had become wary of approaching Mallard. Jem was wondering what could be done when a familiar figure slid down the ladder.

Jem rushed towards Mallard. He backed away, his palm raised.

"No Jemima," he said. "You'd better keep your distance."

A shining tear tracked down Jem's cheek. Her mother's laugh was predictably cold.

"Mother!" cried Jem, rounding on the intruder. "You said you'd developed a treatment."

"Did I say that?" said River, meeting her daughter's eyes with a steely gaze of her own.

"Yes..." snapped Jemima. "You said you had a cure!"

"There's no cure for what he's got," snapped River.

"Mother!" Jem objected.

"Very well," muttered River.

Grudgingly, she reached into her pocket and pulled out two small red bottles. Mallard exercised his right to remain silent, but his eyes never left the little bottles of hope. River rolled them around in the palm of her gloved hand.

"Who stands before you?" asked River. "Florence Nightingale the healer? Or Medea the destroyer of men?"

"Stop babbling," cried Mallard. "Make your blooming mind up!"

River's eyes flashed for an instant before dying down into a contained smoulder.

"Make MY mind up?" she whispered. "No. It's your choice."

She took out two identical bottles.

"You're no Florence Nightingale," hissed Mallard. "You... nightshade!"

Jem watched in horror as Mallard rose like Lazarus and came at his ex-wife like a wounded bull elephant on its final charge. River stepped neatly aside. Mallard lunged forward again, fists flailing.

Tears ran down Jem's face. It had finally happened. There had always been sparks, and the odd worrying incident, (like the harpooning). Jem had been told countless times that people can fight and still love each other. But now her parents were actually trying to kill each other, right here before her very eyes.

"Stop it!" she wailed. Green sparks lit up the cabin like limelight.

"Don't shoot!" cried Jem, pushing past the mercs and stepping in front of their raised tazors. Hass lowered his gun.

"Our daughter has made a wise choice," said River. "Now let's see if you can too. Choose one!"

River backed away towards the ladder, leaving the two bottles on the table.

"Mother! Where are you going?" cried Jem. "We need your help!"

"Sorry Jemima!" said River. "The YPD have left London. You'll be alright."

"I don't understand," said Jem. "If you wanted to kill him, why did you send the shssshter to help us rescue him?"

River's laughter echoed back down the hatchway.

"I sent her with YOU Jem. I told her to keep YOU safe," she called. "I wouldn't have done that if I was a bad mother."

Jem gazed up at the hatch, but she didn't follow her mother.

"Listen love," said Mallard. "Your mother has lost her wits. But there's still a chance I can come through this."

"Half a chance," called River from the hatch above.

Mallard staggered back to the table and picked up one of the bottles. Proudly, Mallard looked at Jem. She glared back at him, her face all puffy and indignant. Here stood a shadow of the unstoppable father she had once known. She would have given anything to get her old dad back. His skin was hanging off his bones. Already the fine lines of the threadneedle disease were spreading like a delicate lacework across his cheek.

Mallard unscrewed the top of the bottle and raised it, ready to drink. Jem gasped, unable to think of what to say. Bitter fumes rose from the glass bottle. Jem gasped as Mallard gulped in a breath and raised the bottle to his cracked lips. And then...

Something stayed Mallard's hand. Most of his decisions were going wrong today. He didn't want Jem to witness the results of a bad choice. There was a fifty percent chance it wouldn't be pretty.

"I'm going upstairs to get some air," he said attempting a casual tone, and walking over to the hatch. Jem watched her father struggle to climb the ladder. Lost in the moment, she could find no words of farewell, so she held her tongue.

Looking around the room, she saw the three mercs unusually silent. The shssshter had moved to the table and was staring at the second red bottle, which stood where River had left it. Leem ran over to it and snatched it up from the table.

"You don't understand," sobbed Jem. "He had to choose one bottle. He took the other one."

But Leem was already climbing the ladder.

"Don't go up there!" yelled Jem fervently.

But Leem wouldn't stop. She shot up the ladder faster than double-struck lightning. Cursing, Jem took off in pursuit of the idiot kid.

Jem didn't know what she expected to find at the top of the ladder, but she knew it wasn't going to be pretty. One bottle had poison, and knowing her mother it was probably the drawn out and painful type rather than the swift-geared variety. Taking in the scene, Jem's eyes quickly settled on the figure propped up against the rail at the back of the boat.

Leem was the first to approach the figure. Jem begged Leem to come back but the child seemed to be acting on a death-wish.

"Wait!" cried Jem. "Don't touch him! It's not safe!"

Mouthing curses, Jem stomped across the wooden deck and stopped next to her father. In his hand he still held the empty bottle. His lips were moving but no sound came from them.

Mallard crashed to the deck like a split mast.

Jem tore the red bottle from her father's lifeless hand.

"Dad! Dad!!" she wailed, as waves of fear pulsed right through her.

Jem looked at her father for the last time, not daring to avert her eyes. She felt that if she looked away, it would crystallize this moment, and make it final. She looked into her father's pale blue eyes. His face was grey and threaded, but the soul's windows were still clear. They were blue and alive, unshrouded by death's veil. Somewhere over the water, a seagull let out a keening cry. Small waves kissed the hull of the boat. Jem called his name again. But whereever Mallard was, he could not hear his daughter's voice.

The moon glowed through the tattered clouds. Waves lapped at the boat. Jem felt the shadow of a woman in a long robe looming over her like a silent river spirit. It was the shssshter, and she was holding the second red bottle in a steady hand.

She gave it a little shake, unscrewed the top and pressed it gently to Mallard's lips. Then she carefully poured its contents into his lifeless mouth. Jem turned away, covering her face. She didn't believe in miracles. Here was a precious life, hanging by a gossamer thread.

Five minutes later, the sleeper awoke: coughing like a baby and clinging to the shssshter like a drowning man on a barrel. Jem was shaking, unable to speak.

"What happened?" asked Hass.

"There were two bottles," smiled Leem. "He needed to drink both of them."

The girl had saved Mallard's life.

Chapter 29: Changes

SREEK'S GLOVED HAND SMASHED INTO THE BELLY OF HIS ENEMY.

"Just clowning," he laughed. Bump thought about smashing his brother's face in and raised his fist. Jem smiled at the mercs. They'd fought each other all the way from London back to the Stormfather island. But it was the friendly sibling violence. Hass had remained aloof, knowing the importance of today's ceremony.

"Ready?" asked Caan. Jem knew he thought she was mad to give away her share to three hundredth of the island's power.

Caan ran his eyes suspiciously along the row of mercs.

"You will be welcome here, as long as you obey our rules," declared Caan.

"You can still change your mind Jem," said Harfleur in a faltering voice. "It's not too late."

"I've made my decision," said Jem quietly.

Caan nodded. Jem unclipped the card from her necklace. Before she could complete the handover, a voice from the back of the hall broke the silence. Jem turned towards the hooded figure. A curtain of amazement swished over Jem's proud eyes.

Hass rounded on the stranger, his eyes bubbling with hot hate. Jem noticed the merc's hand reaching for the tazor that he kept concealed beneath the long leather coat. The mercs had been made to check their weapons at the door, but Hass was expecting something like this to happen and he'd come prepared for trouble.

"So that's it?" said Hass. "You've come here to deny our rightful claim?"

All you could hear in the hall was the rush of the wind outside, railing against the roof. Hass took a step towards the newcomer.

"The only good merc is a dead merc?" he sneered. "Is that what you believe? What do you know of me and my brothers?"
Jem gasped when she saw Hass's hand reaching for the tazor. At the last moment Hass changed his mind.

"How dare you call us liars?" he demanded.

Nick strode confidently towards the angry merc and the crowd melted out of his way like snow on the waves.

"I'm not accusing you mercs of anything," said Nick calmly. "It's these islanders... they're the liars."

Hass stopped in his tracks, disarmed by Nick's revelation.

"What do you mean?" he muttered.

Jem examined the cloaked figure before her. Much of the old YPD swagger had gone, but there was a calm authority about Nick. She liked what she saw. Crossing the floor of the hall, Nick stepped into a pool of torchlight. Jem could see the scars left by the threadneedle. They'd faded slightly but the criss-cross web of veins were still on his face. Jem tried not to stare at the disfigurement but the islanders weren't so considerate.

"Only joking," laughed Nick. "Don't worry. I'm no monster."

Whispers and cries spread around the hall like wildfire.

"Nice," said Jem. "Ever hear that rule about not shouting 'fire' in a crowded hall.

Islanders shuffled towards the door. But Nick's speech wasn't aimed at the islanders. He turned to Harfleur and continued.

"I was infected with a disease," he went on. "I needed help..."

Nick walked slowly over to where Fleur was standing. She hadn't spoken since his arrival. Her face, normally a ghostly pale colour, was turning redder by the second. "But no help came."

"It is our ancient law," said Caan. "The tainted have no place on our island."

"The tainted?" said Nick turning to Harfleur in disbelief. "The tainted?" he said again, recoiling at the word.

Jem rushed towards him. Words flowed into her mouth and when the truth comes, Jem couldn't stop it.

"Listen Caan. Your law was probably invented for good reasons," she said. "The community had no way of dealing with an outbreak of disease. But those reasons don't exist anymore."

Caan stood up, took a pace forward and cleared his throat.

"Would you have us overturn our ancient law?" he asked. His voice was grave. The voice of someone who had already made up his mind.

"We have a vaccine. Enough for everybody," pleaded Jem. Caan looked at her in disbelief. "How is this possible?" he asked.

"He's got a point," said Nick. "Where did you get the vaccine from? Not your mother, surely? She didn't want the YPD to get their hands on it."

"Not from her," explained Jem. "Now we've got ourselves a survivor. And with one survivor we can make antibodies and manufacture as much vaccine as it takes."

Harfleur spoke next, stepping away from Caan and tiptoing towards Jem like a cat stalking a rabbit. For the first time, she looked at Nick, but she could not bring herself to look into his eyes.

Fleur made no reply.

"She's right Fleur," boomed Mallard. "You can change. Change your old laws. They don't work anymore."

Fleur looked at Caan, and then back to Nick. She wanted to change, so badly. But she'd said goodbye to him already, back at the stone house when she lit the candle for him. A tear ran down her cheek, but she could not move her limbs, she was spellbound. The moment was lost.

Harsh shouts rose from the crowd. Voices were raised in anger. Not all the islanders were willing to give up the old laws.

Jem walked slowly over to where Nick was standing and took him by the hand.

"There's nothing to fear," she called. But the islanders were leaving, filing out of the hall, one by one.

Jem saw a pained look flash across Nick's lined face. Harfleur saw it too. As the hall emptied slowly, Harfleur and Caan stood rooted to the spot. Hass and the mercs shuffled uncomfortably.

Jem lent towards Nick, took his hand and kissed his cheek.

"I'm sorry," she said quietly. "I thought they'd be able to handle it."

Nick held Jem in a wordless embrace, but as she buried her face in his chest, he looked over towards the tall girl with the red hair. At least Fleur was looking at him again. She had not turned away. A voice from nearby surprised Jem.

Pulling away from Nick, she turned to the woman in the long flowing robe. Jem saw the marks on her lips where she'd taken out the stitches that had held her mouth speechless for so many years. The voice she spoke up with wasn't old and cracked as Jem had imagined. It was warm and kind - rich like melting butter: the voice was insistent.

"Change your hearts," said the shsssshter again, in a voice growing with confidence.

"She's right", said Nick, turning back towards Jem once more.

156

In the first *London Deep* novel...

Jemima Mallard is having a bad day. First she loses her air, then someone steals her houseboat, and now the Youth Cops think she's mixed up with a criminal called Father Thames. Not even her dad, a Chief Inspector with the 'Dult Police, can help her out this time. Oh – and London's still sinking. It's been underwater ever since the climate upgrade.

ISBN: 978-1-906132-03-3 £7.99

www.londondeep.co.uk

Chosen as a 'Recommended Read' for World Book Day 2011.
One of the *Manchester Book Award's* 24 recommended titles for. 2010.

MØGZILLA

FATHER THAMES

ISBN: 9781906132040 £7.99

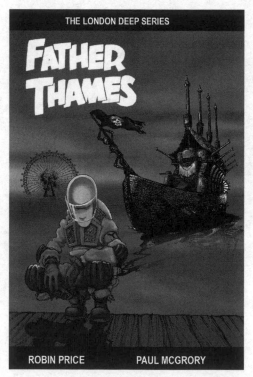

"With non-stop adrenalin-fuelled drama throughout it won't disappoint both new and existing ardent fans of the London Deep series.The mix of text and graphic novel artwork throughout the book adds a further level to the story." – LOVE READING

In Volume 4 of 'London Deep'...
Shami returns from Stormfather island:

MOGZILLA

LONDON DEEP

London Deep (Book 1)
ISBN: 9781906132033 £7.99

Father Thames (Book 2)
ISBN: 9781906132040 £7.99

Threadneedle (Book 3)
ISBN: 9781906132057 £7.99

London Sink (Book 4)
ISBN: 9781906132378 £8.99
ETA: 2018
London Drift (Book 5)
ISBN: 9781906132569 £8.99
ETA: 2019

The *London Deep* series follows the adventures of Jemima
Mallard: the rule-breaking daughter of a policeman whose mother
heads a underground organisation called Father Thames. Told in
a mixture of words and comic art, the story unfolds to reveal how
the failure of the 'Climate Upgrade' wrecked the environment and
drove young people and grown ups apart.

'This is a terrifically atmospheric page-turning adventure told
through words and comic art... a rattling good read and one in which
you are sure to be drawn in to Jem's exploits of survival.'
– *Lovereading.co.uk*

The first London Deep was chosen as a 'Recommended Read' for World
Book Day 2011. One of the *Manchester Book Award's* 24 recommended
titles for. 2010.

www.londondeep.co.uk